SECRET ACQUISITIONS

RALEIGH DAVIS

CHAPTER 1

Fuck me.

I try to pull my breath back into my lungs and my blush back under my skin, but it's too late. Way too late.

I rock back on my heels, nearly tripping over the stilettos. Bad move, terrible move, 'cause then he'll think I dressed up just for this, that I don't wear this getup normally. That I'm usually in sneakers, hoodie, and jeans, the female version of the five jillion brogrammers currently choking the Bay Area.

He'd be wrong. I dress to kill always, whether I'm begging for money, building hardware, or coding like a maniac. The unexpected clothes help when you're one of the few girls breaking into the boys' club of tech.

I need all the help I can get right now, desperate as I am.

The man before me isn't any kind of boy. He was closer to one five years ago, when we were both undergrads at Stanford. He was definitely one that night he made an awkward, nervous pass at me. The pass I shut down. Hard.

Now, with his broad chest, thick arms, and razor jaw, Mark Taylor is all man. The twist to his mouth—half-amused, half-annoyed, all mean—tells me *he remembers.*

He's dressed in what I call rich-dude casual, soft T-shirt clinging to his shoulders and chest, jeans hugging his hips and thighs. Normal enough clothes, but something about the fit and fabric signals they cost more than most people make in a month. The dark chocolate hair and the green eyes—those are the same as in college. He hasn't been able to change everything about himself.

I was doomed the moment I saw him behind the conference table. My calculated risk—that it would be one of his partners instead of him—has blown up in my face.

I'm desperate though, on the run with the hounds on my heels, so I plunge into the thorn patch, not caring if I tear my clothes or skin.

Well, in reality I start my pitch, but I've always had a flair for the dramatic.

"So happy you took this meeting," I murmur, not offering him my hand. Touching him would be a very bad idea. "Let me tell you more about—"

He waves a lazy hand, the gesture dripping with power. Command comes second nature to him now, it seems. "Go back. To what you were talking about before."

"Before?" The only thing I've said is my opening. Unless...

Fuck me. I said "fuck me" out loud.

"Exactly." His smile isn't kind or welcoming, but his voice is a wonder, dripping sex appeal and condescension and making the area between my navel and my knees clench with heat. "I'm more than happy to discuss *that* offer."

"That..." I can play this like that, and I'm almost desperate enough to do it. If Bastard Capital turns me away...

I'm done for. I'll never be able to stop Arne Fuchs, and I'll never find Grace. She's counting on me, and I swore I'd do anything to help her.

If only it weren't Mark Taylor offering. Anyone but him.

This was not the way this meeting was supposed to go.

Yes, I knew Mark was a member of Bastard Capital, him and five other venture capitalists known collectively as the Bastard Boys. How could I not, when *TidBytes* had a story every morning about what Mark and his bros had gotten up to the night before? And the gorgeous women they'd done it with?

But I'd gambled on one of the other Bastards leading this meeting, of having to metaphorically get on my knees with one of them.

Not Mark. Because Mark was going to make it hurt.

I should have walked out the moment I saw him across the wide mahogany conference table. But I was lulled by the bland façade of Bastard Capital, as unassuming as every other venture capital firm on Sand Hill Road. Inside, I was greeted by a Zen garden of a building. There wasn't an actual rock garden—that would have been much too gauche—but every curve, corner, surface, and hallway suggested energy flowing effortlessly.

Maybe it was a metaphor for all the money that seems to flow effortlessly to the Bastards. Money that I need if I'm going to save my friend. And maybe even the whole world too.

"Sorry." I smile like I'm some dumb girl who can't control her mouth. Who knows? After my response, maybe I am. "I didn't mean to say that. Let me tell you about Ultra."

Ultra is my company, my program, and my plan to defeat Fuchs. He's one of the richest men in the world, and I'm only January Harris, obscure programmer and cryptologist, but I have to do something to stop him. Only, I need funds to do that, and the male VC world is notoriously stingy when it comes to female start-up founders. So here I am, begging for money from the one man I swore to never approach.

Mark cuts me off with a wave of his hand, which is surprisingly battered for a man who spends most of his time behind a desk. "I don't want to hear your spiel."

I'm ready for this, because this is what all the VC firms do. You hone a perfect pitch, several sentences that sum up the company and how you'll change the world with it, make up some PowerPoint slides, and then they spend the rest of the meeting pushing you off that pitch, testing you.

They think it's clever, but is it really so clever if they're all doing it?

Only Mark has to be different. I'm expecting some question about undergrad, previous apps I've developed, maybe even my childhood, but Mark doesn't go there.

"I want to talk about the previous offer you made."

My heart pulses because my body wants to talk about that too. And maybe his tongue on my neck and those teeth raking across my nipples.

Shut up, body. Just. Shut. Up.

"I'd rather talk about my start-up." I keep my smile dumb and my voice light. My rejection of him back in college had been anything but.

He'd never believe me, but I've always regretted turning him down. We were friends, and his smiles made me want more. Dinner out, movies, kisses, and one day, maybe even more...

If he smiled like he kissed, it would've been sweet and lovely and exactly what young love should have been.

If I explained to him now why I rejected him, would he even remember? It *had* been all the way back in junior year.

I definitely hadn't forgotten—it was my very first lesson in how tech bros treated women. I didn't want to end up as a cautionary tale, so I told him no, with a sharp harshness I didn't feel, and he never asked again. He stopped smiling at me too.

4

His smile isn't shy or sweet at all now. I could cut myself on the edges of it. But even with the danger, my fingers still itch to touch his lips.

With a hard, choking swallow, I pull myself back together. Remind myself why I'm really here.

And I pull my phone out of my bra.

His gaze is stuck to my hand so hard it will be a miracle if he ever pulls it free. I set the sleek rectangle of glass and electronics on the table and let my fingertips trail over the edges. It's too cold, too slick, but I pretend I'm enjoying it.

I can use his interest in my body to lure him into investing in Ultra. In a single heartbeat, I switch my strategy, tossing my well-honed pitch aside.

"Think about the most intimate thing you own." I let my voice go low, inviting, pulling him toward me as I keep stroking my fingers over the phone. "Something you keep close to you always. Under your pillow, next to your skin, something that holds your entire life. Something you'd never let anyone else touch and you'd be devastated to lose."

He pulls in his top lip with the very tip of his tongue, almost as if reminding himself it's there. Or maybe reminding me. For all that I have his attention, he's still very much in control.

"Is this an app that will let me fuck my phone?"

I'm so surprised I barely catch my laughter. He was funny even before, which was part of his appeal. Only his humor didn't cut so deep then.

"Um, no." I smile because I can't help myself and then try to regain my footing. He's not supposed to make me laugh. "It's encryption software," I say bluntly. I can't be seductive after he's made that joke—I'm just not that good. "Starting with phones, because most people use them for everything. Messaging, photos, phone calls, banking... People aren't joking when they say their lives are in there."

Now imagine someone looking through all that, without your knowledge, using spyware he's implanted on your phone. Selling all that private information to whomever he likes. And you can't do a thing about it.

I can't say that because that someone is Arne Fuchs, tech giant and friend/rival to every other tech giant in the valley, Mark included. They're both major players here in Silicon Valley, and those men—they're *all* men—stick together.

I also can't say anything because Grace wasn't supposed to have access to Fuchs's plans, and she certainly wasn't supposed to pass them on to me.

Mark looks supremely unimpressed, tucking his hands behind his head. His dark gray T-shirt catches on his biceps and holds. I imagine for a moment that my fingers are where the shirt is, cupping his muscles.

"Not many people are interested in encryption," he says. "It's mostly a business-facing thing." With that, he makes a dismissive flick of his fingers.

"But they should be. People don't understand how vulnerable their information is."

"And *you're* going to convince them otherwise?" He raises one strong eyebrow. "People want to assume their banking apps are secure. And everybody already shares everything else on Facebook."

I pounce on that. "Exactly. Shouldn't that *everything* be as secure as it possibly can? And people *are* starting to realize. When someone has their phone hacked or their private pictures strewn all over the internet or when customs asks people to unlock their phone as a matter of routine, people see it could happen to them. Just imagine someone's reaction if their phone was stolen and the thief unlocked it. They'd feel violated, exposed."

I take a moment to let that sink in and to run my fingers down the screen of my phone. Not to be seductive now but to bring home the image of it being broken open, insides exposed.

"But information—your most personal secrets—can be taken without anyone even touching the phone," I say. "We have all these wonderful systems that let us communicate at the speed of light. But they also make us vulnerable. Someone can be inside your phone, and you'd never see them. Never see the person poking through your metaphorical underwear drawer."

His gaze flicks back to my phone, my finger still curled around it. Is he thinking about what I might have inside it? About the intimate secrets locked within?

Or maybe he's thinking about my real underwear drawer, about the pair of lacy panties I put on this morning, black as sin, naughty as a wink, my own personal, secret confidence booster.

Whatever it is, his eyes are dark, bottomless, and so focused as to almost be cruel. I could wither under that intensity if he turned it on me for too long.

"I agree with all that," he says, and my relief is so strong I taste it, sharp and bright like peppermint. "But convincing the average person to care about any of this is impossible."

"Pixio's going to want it." They're the biggest phone manufacturer in the world. And one of the few companies that actually still gives a shit about privacy. "Everyone wants to be customer-facing—the business-facing stuff is getting neglected, and it's ripe for disruption. We're going to be a unicorn."

The unicorns were the white whales of the VC world, the investments that paid off twenty, thirty, fiftyfold. The companies that minted new billionaires when they went big. Every VC was looking for the next unicorn, although most of what they found ended up as duds.

Not everyone got rich in Silicon Valley.

"Everyone who comes in here claims they're a unicorn." Mark shakes his head, the light catching in the sable of his hair. It's shorter now, the curls cut down to simple waves. But the green of his eyes is still the same, soft and mossy.

I mentally slap myself. *Soft? Mossy?* There's nothing soft about the man in front of me. He's hard from his head to his heels and all the many inches between.

Hell, that's even worse since now I'm all tingly and flushed. And he's going to realize that the woman begging him for money—and the girl who once rejected him—is incredibly attracted to him.

"What are you doing Friday?" he asks suddenly.

Do lions play with their food the way cats do? Because that's exactly what this feels like. But a mouse wouldn't be so achingly, arousingly aware of the lion, would she?

I play the dumb blonde even though my hair is black as ink. It's the attitude, not the hair color really. "Why? Do you want to hear my funding pitch then?"

He laughs, all low and rumbly, and I know I haven't fooled him. "No, I want to invite you to a birthday party."

Now I'm confused. Is that part of his revenge too? Why doesn't he just say *Thanks but no thanks, and screw you for rejecting me all those years ago* and send me on my way?

"You want me to come to your birthday party?" I can't remember when his birthday is. We shared a cookie once on his birthday back in college—chocolate chip—but the date is a bit fuzzy.

He rises and comes around the conference table. My knees get wobbly, then give out altogether, the chair behind me catching me. He's coming for me, and all I can do is wait, helpless, breathless, fixed to the chair. My thighs shift, trapped by my tight skirt, and the sensation is so agonizing I close my eyes for half a breath.

One of his fists lands on the table as he braces himself over me. It's intimidating and intimate all at once. My mouth is dry, but my pussy definitely is not.

"It's not my birthday." His amusement is a rough rasp.

My skin quivers in response. "Oh? Then whose?"

"Logan's. It's on Alcatraz." He tosses that out as if it's the Chuck E. Cheese's of billionaire birthday parties.

I don't confess that I've never been there. Alcatraz is for tourists, although apparently it's also for birthday parties. At least for men like him.

"Great," I say. *Wonderful for him. And you.*

It's then I take note of his expression—really study it. His eyes are too dark, his stare too fixed, and his breath just a touch too fast.

Mr. Cool isn't so cool after all.

He's given away more than he planned to here. He might be playing it cool—which I have to admit he's good at—but he wants me. Still.

I can use that.

It can also bite me back. Hard. Because I still want him too, maybe even worse, but my rules from college remain intact. *Don't fuck where you work.*

I'm already in deep shit. I fuck Mark and things get tangled. Fast.

Plus, if he even suspected I'm about to say yes just so I can manipulate him...

Crossing Mark Taylor is the worst idea ever because he will make me pay.

I swallow hard. He'd lean over me just like this, call me a naughty, wicked girl, and give me some terrible punishment.

"I'd love to," I breathe out, hoping he thinks it's attraction that has me all flustered and not this femme fatale scheme I'm cooking up.

Oh, his smile when I say that. It makes me think of pleasing him, of seeing that smile while I'm naked and he is too, and then getting my mind blown for pleasing him so much.

I'm already in danger, and now I'm inviting even more in.

Fuck me.

CHAPTER 2

San Francisco is a wonderful city.

At least it is *if* you're young, wealthy, and unattached—which I most certainly am. This city most of all wants you to have fun, to be chill, to be interesting, exciting… and for a tech billionaire, this city wants those things most of all for *you.*

I'm not in San Francisco right now though—instead, I'm looking at its lights, the rolling glitter of the docks, the beacon of Coit Tower, the thrust of the Transamerica Pyramid, and the spans of the Bay Bridge from across a mile or so of frigid waters. It's a distance meant to impose, to remind me of how far I am from civilization and all the good things in life.

I'm not intimidated though. For tonight my friends and I own Alcatraz.

It was Finn's idea, the redneck of our group. His hobby is racing trucks, dirt bikes, and sand rails as fast as he can over busted-ass dirt roads. People don't take him seriously because of it, which has made him a killer closer in the past. Nobody thinks a redneck has any brains.

Only, we're all so rich and well known now it doesn't fly anymore.

But hell, we can afford to rent Alcatraz for a party, so who cares?

The birthday boy is Logan, the honeypot of the group. He hates it when we call him that, so naturally it stuck. But yeah, flies on honey—that's Logan with the ladies.

He's got at least three around him right now, all of them looking more than eager to accompany him home. Good. He needs to enjoy himself, especially this birthday.

I raise my glass to him across the yard, the wind screaming outside the window. It's loud enough to pierce the music throbbing through the place. I can only imagine how horrifying the wind must sound all on its own.

Logan raises his glass back, then raises his eyebrows.

You're alone, that look says. *Want me to help you find some company?*

I shake my head. I'm waiting for someone in particular tonight. Someone I have no plans of sharing with anyone, at least not until I'm done with her. The second she walked into the conference room, it was a done deal. Even if she didn't know it.

Dev, our math genius, marches up to me, looking pissed. I'm surprised he actually came—this is definitely not his scene.

"What happened with the Ultra meeting?" he yells into my ear.

I'm the front of the house for our little group of VCs. Pressing flesh, interrogating applicants, leaning on people who are trying to fuck us over—I can be a good cop or a bad cop or both at once. Whatever we need when it comes to manipulating people.

Except I lost my vaunted cool with January Harris. I hadn't meant to—I'd told myself it was only going to be a pitch meeting. Not between old friends—we certainly were not fucking that—but between businesspeople. You didn't have to like everyone you did business with, and most of the time, I didn't. Her prospectus was interesting, and she was building a reputation as a brilliant coder, ready to make the leap to the big time. A good, solid investment and nothing more.

And then she said *fuck me* and my dick said *hell yes.* The rest of me did too.

I've played this game before with January, five years ago, only it wasn't a game to me then. I was madly in lust with her, had been for two years, and was a huge fucking dork. I can admit it. One day I worked up the nerve to ask her out.

She told me it would never happen. Not ever.

I'd been turned down by girls before then—and after, but not for very long, not once we'd started to make money—but January's rejection was the one that haunted me. Maybe because of all the girls I asked out, she was the one who mattered the most. When I asked her if she wanted to grab a drink, see a movie, she smiled back for almost two heartbeats. I know. I counted. It was the smile I'd always dreamed of seeing from her.

And then her eyes had gone hard as diamonds and she'd said, *No, not ever.*

I'm going to relish saying that exact thing to her when she begs me to fuck her for real this time.

I say none of that to Dev since he'd disapprove.

"I need more time to go over their numbers," I say smoothly, and it isn't entirely a lie. "I wasn't impressed."

That was a lie. January had been dressed in some tight skirt that went past her knees, all innocent from the front and with a slit almost up to her ass in the back, a flash of sweet, tender knee and thigh peeping at me with every step as I'd walked her to the door. I wanted to tear the slit open all the way to her hips, bend her over the conference table, and bury myself in her pussy.

You could have definitely called me impressed.

"Really?" Dev's expression shifts like he knows I'm hiding something. "Logan spoke highly of her architecture."

My fist curls before I realize Dev is talking about software architecture and not her curves.

"I want to get Paul's opinion too."

Paul is one of the other Bastards, the one who thinks all this joking posturing is nonsense. Well, so does Dev actually, but Dev treats it the way a robot might an annoyance: something to be ignored until it interferes with his programming. Paul will laugh even as he rolls his eyes.

Paul, the man himself, walks up then, his cheeks red. I can't tell if it's because he's been drinking—he gets the "glow"—or if it's because it's fucking freezing here by the windows. This place must have been agony for the prisoners, with the wind screaming outside and the cold sinking into every corner.

And we'd chosen it for a birthday party. Call it living up to our reputation. We take ourselves much less seriously than the rest of the tech world with all their bullshit about disruption and changing history and culture-altering paradigms. Silicon Valley needs the six of us to give it the finger when we could, if only as a protest.

"You don't need to wait for Paul's judgment," Dev says.

"Dev doesn't trust me?" Paul grabs his heart. "I'm wounded. Where did our love go?"

"Fuck you," Dev says and walks off, because he's sure as shit got "Tainted Love" stuck in his head now. He's more susceptible to earworms than anyone I know. It's one of his few human qualities.

"Charming as always," Paul says. "And no, I haven't looked

at the Ultra prospectus yet. I was waiting for your report on the meeting."

She told me to fuck her, so I invited her here. That's the summary of that meeting.

Except I'm lying to myself. Because she was scared too. Terrified. And trying so hard to hide it.

She was right about everyone's information being vulnerable, and I was right about the average Joe not giving a shit. But her fear was personal, which I couldn't figure out. A coder as talented as January could lock down her shit, no problem.

What the hell had her so spooked? I was going to find out. Mostly because I was curious and also because I didn't like seeing her scared. Her vulnerability still got to me.

She's rejected you before, dude. Don't fall for her now.

"I haven't come to a recommendation on that," I say mildly to Paul because I'm not going to betray January's secrets even if she didn't mean for me to see them. "Do we ever not talk about work these days?"

Paul ponders that. "Finn and I were at the urinals together the other day, and I asked what it was like having a dick so small you needed an electron microscope to see it. Does that count?"

"What did Finn say?"

"Nothing. But he somehow managed to get into my office and rearrange all the furniture so it was a mirror image of before. The desk was blocking the door—I had to get Maintenance to take the thing off its hinges to get in—so I have no idea how he did it."

Finn does love his elaborate pranks, something he picked up at Caltech. I always wondered what the nerds there thought of that dirtbag redneck rolling into those hallowed halls.

But then I stop thinking of nerds and college and even Paul because January is walking in.

The eighties are having a revival right now, all over January's tight dress. It's like a second skin, slinky and tight, outlining every curve. Every curve I'd like to run my tongue over. Her heels are fuck-me inches high, and the sharp points of them will feel amazing digging into the small of my back when she wraps her legs around me.

"You found it," I say to her as she slides up, her hips swishing in a way that makes my dick twitch.

And then I catch sight of who's with her and my mood goes as dark and cold as the bay.

"What the fuck?" I growl. Not at her but at Julian Groves, who's got a hand at her back and is wearing a smile that makes me want to take his teeth out with my knuckles.

"Shit," Paul says on a breath from beside me, more circumspect than I am. "How did he get here?"

The more important question is, has Logan seen? And can we pitch Julian off this rock before he does?

I cross my arms over my chest. "The ferry's back the way you came."

January pauses, her cheeks going dark. Yeah, she knows she's done something very bad. "Julian wanted to discuss some business, and he was only free tonight, but I had this..."

Everyone in the valley knows you can deal with the Bastards or you can deal with Julian—but the Bastards and Julian do not do deals together. If you approach one of us for capital, forget approaching the other.

I'd say it's nothing personal, but it very much is.

"Great party," Julian says. "I mean, some people might think renting out Alcatraz is a bit much..."

Like any of us give a fuck about that. But I say nothing because I'm still figuring how to play this—good cop or bad cop. I did bad cop with that ferry line completely by accident.

His hand on January fried my common sense like a cheap resistor.

Then it hits me: Julian's being smarmy, so I'm going to outdick him.

"All the money is going to the Park Service," I say, mirroring his shitty smile back to him. "We think it's a good cause." I turn to January, letting my smile carry a warning now. "But we're here to celebrate, not talk business."

She goes pale, the wind whipping her hair into her face and catching on her cherry-red lips.

My dick twitches again.

Yeah, this invitation wasn't about business. It's about the attraction between us and why she turned me down in college. It's clear now why she's attracted to me—money is better than any number of hours in the gym.

I'd just thought January was better than that. It's unfair that I'm toying with her like this, but I've reached a point where I don't have to be anything I don't want to.

I don't want to be fair. I want her in my bed.

By bringing Julian, she's not playing fair either. I didn't expect her to, but my competitive urge—and my cock—is raring to go, to show her who's in charge here.

Before I can diffuse the Julian situation, Paul walks up, blocking Julian from the rest of the party, going for the physical approach. "Come on, man. You know you shouldn't be here."

It's too late though. Logan's charging up, his expression stark, wild-eyed.

Fuck, fuck, fuck. And there's a reporter from *TidBytes* watching the whole thing. Logan's in that gossip rag every damn day, mostly with a woman on his arm. A mug shot would not be a great addition to their collection.

"Is Callie with you?" Logan demands, all clenched jaw and tight fists.

The atmosphere is charged with tension and threaded with sadness. Logan shouldn't have to deal with this on his birthday. I wanted him to have fun, to finally forget Callie for a while.

Julian rolls his eyes, and I can't blame him, because why would Logan's ex-wife come to his birthday party? Yeah, she did leave him for Julian, but even Callie wouldn't pull that.

"She's not." Julian's tone is flat, almost pissed—pretty ballsy of him considering he stole Logan's wife.

Maybe Callie's left him too. Which is no less than he deserves.

Logan sags, but his shoulders are squared and his fists are up, like he's going to pop Julian one.

Time to swing in and pretend everything's A-OK even though I want to drag January off to the nearest corner and explain why this was a very bad idea and demand what exactly she's going to do to make it up to me.

After. I'll do that after.

"Julian." I'm handing the knife to him handle first here, but if he pisses me off, I'll reverse it right quick. "Didn't you want to talk to Paul?"

Paul can haul off Julian, I'll talk down Logan, and then I can get back to January. But Julian's got to cooperate here.

Julian takes my offered blade and puts it into his smile, sharp and knowing all at once. "Sure. I'd *love* to talk to Paul."

Paul sends me a look. *Thanks, asshole.* But he drags Julian off because that's what we do. We have each other's backs.

Julian fucked Logan—his wife, to be precise—so we'll fuck him back every chance we get.

"Logan." I whack him on the back, both to snap him out of it and provide support. "It's your party, man. Forget that asshole, grab a drink, enjoy yourself."

He nods, but I can tell his mood is ruined. Yes, the ladies

flock to him, and yes, he encourages them, but in the end, he's still not over Callie. It's a goddamn shame, if you ask me.

I push him back toward the party, hoping he finds a better mood in there. I'm worried about him and want to follow—but first I need to deal with January.

When I turn to her, I'm wearing my best smile. My smile that says *I'm going to be the good cop here, but I'm still a cop. I'm still in charge.*

January's eyes are wide, her mouth a perfect O.

"You know the rules about Julian and us," I say, smooth as molten glass. "What did you think you were doing?"

Her expression closes. The surprise is gone, and she's ready to deflect again.

Too bad. I like her surprised face. I'll have to arrange to see it again.

"Julian wanted to meet tonight," she says, all cool composure. "I'm not rich"—*Like you,* the tilt of her eyebrow says —"so I can't leave any source of funds on the table. I invited him along. After all, it's only a birthday party."

She's not wrong, but something possessive surges in me anyway. Maybe because she's not even a bit afraid here, which hits me with a fist of arousal so strong I want to go to my knees and drag her down with me.

But still, Julian is a no-go. "You think your encryption scheme is good enough to have me overlook this?"

She tips her head, coy. "Isn't it?"

"Are you trying to make me jealous?"

"Of course. Purely in a business sense."

What a tease. I'm charmed and annoyed in equal measures since she didn't come here in that dress with Julian on her arm purely for business.

"Want a drink?" I ask.

She takes in the rows of cells, the wind whistling outside

the window, and the edged chill seeping through the windows. "This doesn't seem like the place for a birthday."

I find myself agreeing with her, especially now it's only the two of us in the solitary block. I want us to be someplace warm and dark, a place meant for pleasure rather than torture.

"We can afford it," I say, then feel like a complete dick. I hate that feeling, because she should be the one on edge here, not me.

"Right." She's more sad than anything. Then she forces herself to smile. "Should we grab that drink and discuss my prospectus?"

It's the last thing I want to do. I want to know why she's sad now, why she was afraid before, what brought her to my door for funding. Yes, I run one of the biggest VC firms in the valley, but January would never have come to me if she wasn't desperate. I know that much about her.

"Sure." I gesture her into the main hall where the DJ and bar and food and dance floor are set up. Even we knew setting up a party atmosphere in the solitary block would be too much, so we kept that area empty. As we head toward a table, I ask, "What can I get you?"

Wine, I'm guessing. Something as red as her lipstick but not nearly as heady and lush as her kisses would be. She'd sip from a glass with a sensual loop of her wrist, leaving behind an impression of her lips on the rim.

Jesus, I haven't even touched her and I'm already losing myself in fantasies, just like I used to in college.

She turns to me with a slight smile, her hair falling forward over her shoulder. The urge to push it back is almost unstoppable. She has to lean in so I can hear her, and I put a hand to her elbow, helping her move closer. Her mouth opens, and I can taste the mint on her breath—

Stiffness suddenly grips her, turning her into a statue of fear. She's terrified again.

I spin to see what's frightened her, my hand still on her elbow and my blood rising for a fight. Okay, I'm not exactly feeling charitable toward her, but whoever's put that look on her face needs to be dealt with.

I don't see anyone but the crowd though. No one's staring back at her, and I don't see anyone who doesn't belong. It's the cream of the valley before us, the richest, most powerful, most innovative people in the world. No one who would threaten her.

But she's definitely frightened. The fact that I can't see why makes the hair on my neck stand up.

"January?" I'm not playing any kind of game here. I'm truly worried about her.

She blinks, forces her expression to blankness. The effort in it quivers in the delicate skin around her eyes. "Actually, could we get out of here?"

We. This is my opening. Yes, she wants my money, and I want her, but there's a middle ground between those points. We can explore that ground tonight.

I wait, in case someone—whoever's spooked her—comes up, says hello.

But we remain alone, and her impassive expression never breaks. I smile although I don't mean it. "Sounds good. There's a ferry leaving in five minutes. And I've got a car waiting."

One car for the two of us. I can tell she catches my meaning by the way she blinks, her surprise and yes, pleasure, slipping through the cracks in her calm.

"Great." She doesn't mean her smile either.

At least we're on the same page here.

CHAPTER 3

January

The night is cold and smeared with fog, typical for a San Francisco evening. The lights of the city bleed yellow, orange, and red into the mist, turning everything into a hyperactive impressionist landscape.

But all that is outside the car, unable to penetrate the warm luxury of the back seat of the hired car. A girl could get used to this.

I look over at Mark, who *is* used to this. "A car and a driver?" I raise an eyebrow, mocking him in an attempt to gain the higher ground here. Or at least regain my footing.

Seeing Arne Fuchs at the party shook me hard. I should have expected him to be there, but it still rattled me. For a long, horrifying moment, I thought he might have followed me.

But of course he hadn't. He'd send one of his minions to do that.

"I usually drive myself," Mark says. He's not at all put off, and the way he says *special* makes me think he got the car just for me. My savior of the evening, spiriting me away when I'd seen a ghost. "Tonight's special."

"Can you give him my address? It's in the Outer Sunset—"

"We're going to my place."

"I never said…"

He lets the pause lengthen until my nerves are as stretched as the silence is. "You could have called a Lyft, hailed a cab, even caught the Muni. But you got in this car. With me. We both know what that means."

He's trying to intimidate me, and it's working. But it's not a scary intimidation—it's one filled with taut longing and scratchy need.

Still, I resist. "Is this all part of your act? Your super alpha billionaire act? Let me guess: you've got an entire room of sex toys at home you want to introduce me to."

"It's no act. And I don't need toys to fuck."

Jesus. My breath leaves me in a wave of heat, because no, he most certainly doesn't. He'd probably have a woman screaming and begging just with that rock-hard body of his.

My eyes dart to the front of the car where the driver is staring straight ahead.

"He didn't hear," Mark says. "If we're quiet, he won't hear anything."

But he might see if he happened to glance back, me on my knees, my mouth buried in Mark's crotch—the image I now can't get out of my head.

"This is highly inappropriate," I try. I don't know if I'm telling him or me.

It bounces right off him. "Says who? Is there some ethics committee watching us? This has nothing to do with the Bastards funding you. When it comes to business, I don't think with my dick."

He's insulted now, spitting that out. I glance at his crotch, the fabric pulled taut by his erection. He might not think with his dick, but it definitely has some ideas of its own.

I point to his cock with a courage I don't actually feel. "So this isn't business then?"

He shifts in the seat, his erection straining even harder. "No. This is you and me and the fact that you want me inside you as badly as I want to be there."

It's true—I do want him to fuck me. I'm vibrating with the need to feel him fill me, stretch me, grind into me with desperation. The confrontation with Julian and my shock at seeing Fuchs has supercharged my nerves. I'm gasoline-soaked, and Mark is a lit match.

"And tomorrow?" I ask softly. "And after that, when I'm back in your offices asking for money?"

"Tonight is tonight," he says. "And tomorrow is tomorrow." As if it's just that simple.

"So tomorrow it's over? Done?" But I don't like that notion—my muscles tighten in protest. My body wants more than only one night.

"If you want." There's nothing casual about that—he's not being cool with it being a one-night stand. Interesting.

The Mark Taylor I knew in college would have been all about forever—there were long walks on the beach, brunches, and puppies in his eyes then.

This Mark doesn't have any of that in his eyes. But he also isn't pushing for a short-term fling.

I don't know what to make of it, and it scares me.

My rule has always been to never date where I work, although Mark isn't exactly offering a date here. Without asking, I already know he doesn't have any rules. He's a man and rich enough to weather any storm. But even when he was broke and a student, it was different for him.

It wasn't different for Chloe when she slept with Jake our second year. Being a woman in the computer science program was like being chum among a feeding frenzy of sharks. One smell of blood and they all wanted a bite.

Chloe slept with Jake, and then she broke up with him. Kevin asked her out after that; she turned him down.

But Kevin felt like he was owed. Chloe had offered herself to Jake—therefore Kevin wanted a bite too. And Jake was angry that she'd left him.

Pictures appeared on the CS undergrad email loop, of Chloe naked and bound, on her knees with Jake. It spread like a sewage spill after that, nasty, foul rumors appearing on Facebook and horrible, photoshopped pictures popping up on Twitter.

By the time Kevin and Jake and the rest of their friends were done with her, Chloe had to drop out of school.

And I learned that if you want to swim with sharks, you have to be inedible. Untouchable.

Only for women though. It's always different for the men, although Mark wouldn't understand that.

"Tomorrow is never just tomorrow," I say. "Today bleeds into tomorrow in so many ways." Ways that he'll never understand, protected as he is by his money and his gender.

"You only want your funding then." The temperature inside the car drops as low as it is outside.

"Everyone here wants funding. You should know that better than anyone."

"I'm not talking about everyone. I'm talking about you."

The way he says that puts the rest of the world into soft focus, with me as the sharp, defined center of his attention.

I can't have him looking too closely into my motives though. "What about you?" I ask. "You didn't used to be like this."

He doesn't pretend to misunderstand, which is a relief. We've got enough brewing between us without adding polite lies. "Neither did you. How did you get into encryption? Why this for your first start-up?"

This isn't my first company, but that's not what he means. I've worked for plenty of start-ups already, a few that did okay, more that crashed and burned. He means why this for my first stab at running everything myself? Why did I decide to take my chance on this?

"I've always liked puzzles. Crossword puzzles, logic puzzles, anything tricky that my mind has to unravel."

"I remember that. I tried to help you once with a crossword. It was a disaster."

I laugh, because I remember too. The two of us in a computer lab, everyone else tapping away while we bent our heads together over something so old-fashioned. "That was a *New York Times* Sunday crossword. Those are tough."

"You finished it." His expression is too deeply assessing to really be appreciative. "Without cheating or asking for help. I remember that too."

I shrug uncomfortably because his tone is one I can't parse. Is he upset that I was good at them? Does he admire it? I can't tell at all. "Encryption and puzzles go hand in hand. In each instance, you take some information, scramble it according to a particular pattern, and then reassemble it at some point."

In the end, encryption is just making a puzzle that no one else can solve. Not even a computer.

I'm hoping to make a puzzle that Fuchs's spyware will never solve. One that will prevent him from looking into people's most private secrets.

"What about you?" I ask. Enough about me. Letting him get too close would be a mistake here even if we do sleep together. Sex is one thing. Secrets are another entirely. "I wouldn't have guessed you'd end up as a VC."

He'd struck me as someone more like myself, interested in algorithms and designing hardware—all more esoteric stuff that you did for the sheer joy of it. I don't know him that well anymore, but I get the impression he doesn't have much sheer joy in his life these days. Yeah, not everyone can have a birthday party at Alcatraz, but he wasn't exactly enthused by the place.

"You've probably already heard the story."

Yeah, the media loved to retell it, because it was such a perfect calculation of the American dream: one part skill, one part determination, with a hefty dose of luck. A group of six friends get together to create an algorithm to predict stock prices. They plan to sell it to some Wall Street firms if it works well enough. Only it ends up working so well they get rich just off the testing phase when the stock buys they made to test the algorithm end up making millions.

Yep, they were modern-day fairy tales come to life. Now they spend their days betting on the next big thing, nurturing the firms that will be the future of the valley.

It's a great story, an awesome story. But it still doesn't quite explain how Mark got here. Stock-price predictions seem too banal for him.

"I know that you and Paul were good friends at Stanford," I say. The Paul of today definitely fits with the Paul I'd known back then. His family is business royalty in Singapore, and the path to where he was now seemed pretty straightforward. Of course he'd want a magic program to see into the future of the stock market. "How did you meet the rest of them?"

He shrugs as if the six of them coming together was pretty ordinary and not a crazy twist of fate. "Paul knew Logan from some machine-vision project they both worked on. Logan and Finn went to Caltech together. And Elliot is Logan's brother."

Oh yes, Elliot the lawyer. Not a programmer, not an engineer, but still a Bastard. I hadn't seen him at the party, but he never appeared in *TidBytes* like the rest of them. He must be too busy doing lawyerly stuff.

"And Dev?"

I was only asking the question everyone in the valley wanted to know—who was Dev and where had he come from? The profiles never gave any information about his family or where he'd grown up. They did mention that he'd gone to Cal State Fullerton—not exactly a tech powerhouse —and that he was the brains behind their magical stock-trading algorithm.

None of the Bastards had ever confirmed exactly which of them had written it. They'd always insisted it was a group effort.

"Dev is Dev." Mark smiled crookedly as if to say *I'm as puzzled by him as you are.*

The atmosphere between us shifts, still sizzling hot, still charged, but more comfortable as well. I'm horribly aware of him and my own body, but I'm also enjoying talking to him.

"A man of mystery, huh?" I smile back, because it is a little silly in this day and age for a grown man to spring up from nowhere. The internet knows all and sees all, except when it comes to Dev.

Arne Fuchs might know who he is though. He might have peered into those dark corners of the internet, the ones the reporters don't even think to search, and found out every-thing there is to know about Dev. Especially the stuff Dev clearly doesn't want others to find out.

Shudders run over me even though I'm warm and safe inside the car. Mark catches it, and his frown is protective, concerned.

"What spooked you at the party?" he asks.

Everything's blurred, confused, cold as I struggle to answer. I still don't know if Mark and Fuchs are friends or even business associates, but they're close enough to be dangerous to me. And to Grace.

"Was it Julian?" he asks when I don't answer.

My anxiety pops so fast I want to laugh from the release

of the pressure. He's jealous. Yes, I know that Julian and the Bastards have bad blood—tech people are as gossipy as anyone else—but the only thing I want from Julian is funding. Honest.

Even more honest: I want more than just funding from Mark.

"No, it wasn't Julian." I wasn't a bit guilty about leaving Julian behind without even a wave—given his shit-eating grin when Logan went after him, I'm guessing he said yes to my invite more to fuck with the Bastards than to hear my pitch.

Mark leans back against the seat, but it's too late. He's already given himself away. I ought to be triumphant since he's more vulnerable than he's letting on, but instead I'm relieved. And happy.

"Then who was it?" he asks. "You looked really scared."

He sounds like he wants to track the guy down and make absolutely certain he can never scare me again.

"I thought I saw someone who wasn't there."

If that works, I can't tell, because the car is coming to a stop. We're on a street lined with beautiful homes behind high gates, right in the heart of the Marina. I can see the bay from here, the boats in the harbor, the dark mass of Marin, and even the Golden Gate Bridge, its lights almost as pretty as the starlight. This view alone must be worth several million.

This isn't Millionaires' Row—this is Multi*Billionaires'* Row.

"Sir," the driver says from the front.

How much has he heard? And how much is Mark paying him not to hear?

"January." Mark's voice is low, quiet in the idling car. Almost gentle. "You still have a choice." He opens the door, slides out, then offers me his hand.

If I shut the door on him, the driver will take me wherever I want to go. I don't have to stay here.

But if I shut the door on him, we're done. No nights together, no funding.

The fact that I think of the funding second startles me.

I'm in serious trouble with not one but two powerfully wealthy men after me. Only, Mark isn't pursuing me to bring me down. At least not to any place beyond his bed.

If I take his hand, agree to enter his house, his world, I'm only ensnaring myself in something I may never be able to twist out of. I should say no. Keep it professional between us. Cold.

Except I'm not cold at all. I'm aflame, because I *need* him. In every sense of the word.

So I take his hand and let him pull me from the car. And I send up a little prayer that somewhere in this hard, intense man is the college boy who used to smile so sweetly at me.

CHAPTER 4

My house is filled with beautiful things. Sleek, fine, and worth every penny I paid for them.

I don't say that to brag. Because despite all the luxury surrounding her, there is nothing more gorgeous than January stalking through my living room. The windows overlooking the bay frame her with the ink-dark water and the light dancing across it, the Golden Gate stretching from the City to Marin. It's a setting that's perfectly made for her, a diamond amid all that glitter.

I should be remembering that she brought Julian to our party, causing a scene, and that the only reason she walked into Bastard Capital was because of the money.

But then I have to remember the frisson of fear running through her as she gave her pitch and her very real, very naked fright tonight.

There was also her tender smile as she remembered doing the crossword together all those years ago. I thought I'd feel nothing but cold satisfaction at getting her here, but the past is more potent than I'd realized. Dangerously so, the same as January herself.

"Is that a real Miró?" she asks, pointing to the painting on the wall.

I shake my head. "My cousin is an artist. That was from her surrealist class. All the stuff here is hers—she's very prolific."

"And talented."

January has no idea. Everything I've got is merely Joan's castoffs—the real stuff is sitting down in a gallery in Union Square, being snapped up by my tech peers. But I like having this slightly off art in my home, chosen not to show how big my wallet is or what cutting-edge taste I have but pieces more real to me than any multimillion-dollar canvas could ever be.

January sends me a tilted, teasing grin, and my heart is jolted. This feels so damn real, like we're picking up from where we should have left off in college. Or maybe I only want it to be that real.

She's here for her company. For the money. I might be a charming motherfucker, but she's also desperate.

And frightened. My heart jolts again. She never did say what spooked her, because it wasn't any damn ghost. No, it was something—or someone—all too real.

"Has she ever painted you?" January asks.

I answer her smile, because she's going to love this. "Yeah." I motion her forward into the hallway that leads to my office. The mahogany double doors are wide open, my antique banker's desk framed between them, forlorn in its massive majesty among all that sleek modernist crap.

The top is green felt, and the feet and drawers are carved with griffons and vines. It's a desk that belongs to an entirely different era, and I love it.

January immediately gasps at the sight. "Where did you find this?"

"In the East Bay at some random furniture store."

She runs her fingers over the felt, bends over to inspect the carvings, throwing herself into exploring my desk.

I've never had sex on this desk or any desk; it's just too damn clichéd. But suddenly I want to bend January over, pull up that tight skirt of hers while leaving those killer heels on, and sink fully into her.

Wait, scratch that. I want her sitting on the desk instead, her legs spread wide and me between her thighs, tasting her. Driving her wild.

I can almost imagine how she'll smell, musky and sharp, thick with desire. The sensation is so real, so forceful, my hand starts to shake. I curl it into a fist and tell it to behave. I've given a lot of women oral sex—I'd even call myself pretty fucking good at it—but only January threatens to bring me to my knees before I've even begun.

I'm supposed to be the one in control here, and instead I want to surrender to my need before I've even touched her.

"So where is this picture?"

Her question pulls me out of my fantasy and back into the moment. I point to it. "My cousin said that every successful man needs an oil painting of himself. So she decided to gift me with this."

January starts to laugh, putting her fingers over her mouth to hold it in. Her entire face lights up, bright enough to see in the dark.

I can't blame her for laughing—the painting is of me at twelve, wearing a *Star Wars* T-shirt, shorts, and white socks up to my knees, standing in front of a computer. The style is garishly cartoonish, but my cousin has painted me with such a happy expression that it's clear she's making fun of me out of love.

It's probably my favorite painting in the entire world, one that I don't let many people see. Not everyone would see the affectionate humor in it, and even more would take it as a blow to my ego. I'm supposed to be one of the most powerful men in one of most powerful industries in the world; pictures like that of me shouldn't exist.

But January knew me before, rejected me before. Even if she's only here because of the money, I knew she would appreciate it.

There are so few people in my life who would.

"That painting is amazing," she gets out between laughs. "It actually looks a lot like you in college."

"Please don't remind me what a dork I was back then."

It's as if lightning strikes between us, snapping us back into our respective corners when I say that. Reminding us of the distance and antagonism that should be between us. Even though I know this is the way things should be—me on the offensive, her on her toes—I still miss the easy warmth once it's gone.

"I won't then," she says quietly. "But thank you for showing it to me."

She takes a step back and folds her hands, her entire body saying *what do you want me for next?*

The answer is crystal clear, always has been, but my conscience pulses like a stubbed toe.

"You can still go home." *There*, I tell my conscience, *she's not a prisoner. She can do whatever she wants.*

She lifts her chin, and she looks like the January I remember from college. Brave and wicked smart and ready to take on the world. "I don't want to."

My aching conscience surrenders to a warm, glad rush of relief. Time to celebrate this victory with a special treat.

I crook my finger at her, never saying a word, letting my expression describe the depth of my desire for her. She comes easily enough to stand before me, but her pulse is fluttering in her throat, a butterfly trying to escape its containment.

34

She reaches behind her to unfasten her dress, and I shake my head. That's not what I have planned.

"On the desk." My voice is rougher than I want it to be. I need to remember my control here.

She pushes the chair out of the way and spreads her fingers wide on the green felt, letting her head rest between her outstretched arms. Her ass, pushed high in the air by her skyscraper stilettos, tilts up invitingly.

"Like this?"

It looks so damn hot I'm tempted to abandon my original plan. When I come around behind her, I see that her dress has ridden up high enough to reveal the lace edges of her stockings and the tiniest sliver of bare thigh. I sink my fingers in her hips and pull that gorgeous ass toward me, grinding my cock against her. Even through several layers of clothes, the sensation is wildfire licking my skin.

Oh yes, I could very much do it like this. But somehow, even with the pure lust boiling in my veins, something's off. Not quite in the right place.

Her. She's not where I want her to be.

I steady my grip on her hips and, with an easy flick, turn her toward me and set her ass on the desk. Her legs open naturally, invitingly, and I step between them. Her skirt is clinging just barely to her upper thighs, ready to give up all her secrets with the slightest tug.

Rather than taking advantage, I kneel before her. Immediately her scent hits me, more complex and enticing than I'd hoped. I'd bet my entire fortune she's already soaked her panties.

She's definitely already shocked, her eyes wide and her mouth a wicked, hot *O.* My cock pulses at the sight. *Later. There'll be time later.*

For right now my plan is to keep on shocking her. I slip a hand under her skirt, finding the tops of her stockings. The lace gives way to the satin of her skin, and I toy with the edges, watching her pant with every motion of my fingers.

"These are very naughty." I tug one stocking down until the lace catches at the top of her knee. "Do your panties match?"

Her cheeks flood with pink, and she catches the edge of her lip with her teeth, delicious guilt written all over her.

"Oh," I say slowly. "Oh, you were very naughty."

"The dress is too tight for panties," she gets out.

I'd call it perfectly tight, and sure enough, when I slide my hand higher, there's no barrier between me and her soft curls. I delve deeper and find the core of her. Her folds are slick and plump, swollen with need.

I can't see anything, only feel, which might be a good thing. If I could see my fingers tracing her pussy lips, see her moisture coating my skin, see how hot and wet and flushed she was, I'd completely lose control. I'm barely hanging on as it is, the floor seeming to vibrate beneath my knees.

No, that's not the floor vibrating—that's all of me, eager to get at her, to devour her with pleasure. I shouldn't be this keyed up, not this soon, not with simply touching her, but I am.

Thank God she doesn't seem to notice, with her head thrown back, her lip between her teeth, and her hips giving small jerks. She's more lost in this than I am, although the expression on her face, the stark, needy line of her throat, threatens to pull me all the way under.

Keep it cool, Taylor. Remember why she's doing this.

Because she fucking wants me as much as I want her, my libido snarls back.

"Open your thighs," I command, my fingers still teasing all her most sensitive spots, the ones that make her breath catch.

Her legs shake as if on marionette strings, the instructions from her brain garbled by her pleasure. But slowly she gives me one inch, then two. Her skirt rucks up past her hips.

The change has transformed her pussy into the most enticing peep show, with her dark curls revealing and concealing her lips and clit as she shifts, seeking more sensation. She's hooked her heels into the drawer handles, the better to hold on. And the better to expose herself to me.

I'd thought the desk was perfect when I bought it, but it hasn't achieved true perfection until now, with this woman framed on its surface.

I don't care what brought her into my VC firm in this moment; I'm too damn thankful she came at all.

I sink my fingers into her thighs, steadying myself and her. Things are going to get wild here. Then I lower my head and taste her.

My first taste is a gentle one; I want to savor her, to get to know her desire. I was right—her juices aren't sweet at all. They're musky, earthy, and tangy with need. Beautiful.

I lick again, taking in all of her pussy, all the way to her clit. Her thighs tremble under my hands. This time her taste is deeper, more encompassing. My cock pulses, sensing exactly where it ought to be.

On my next pass, I linger over her sensitive spots, the ones I already know make her weak. Her thighs tremble, then strain, and her breathing goes harsh and guttural. This is a rough, demanding need taking over her.

But then I'm a rough, demanding man.

I circle with the very tip of my tongue, moving closer and closer to her clit, pushing her harder and harder. When I finally make contact with the swollen, straining bud, January jerks like a live wire. The desk creaks as her heels dig in. Her knees are pressing hard against my hands, urging me on.

I don't need to be told twice. I slip one, then two fingers inside her, finding the spot where all her nerve ends are waiting for me. With my hand working in concert with my tongue, I push her to a fever pitch. I can't see her expression, but the moans she's making—rough, achy, begging—tell me she's utterly lost in what I'm doing to her. Hell, I'm halfway to lost myself, simply from soaking in her responses.

Her pussy clenches tight around my fingers, again and again, her climax setting a new rhythm between us as her hips lift completely off the desk.

"Oh hell, oh hell, oh hell," she chants. I wish it was my name she was calling, but we'll get to that. I'll make certain of it.

I get to my feet as all of her goes limp, her orgasm leaving her a boneless sprawl. Her dress is around her waist, her legs hanging over the edge of the desk, and her lungs gasping for air. A tendril of hair clings to her sweat-slick face, but she doesn't brush it away. Maybe her arms aren't working again yet.

Never in my life have I seen anything more gorgeous. I want to tear open my fly and bury myself in her, just like this.

And then I want to gather her up and put her in my bed.

I'm definitely going to do one, but not the other. Because gorgeous as she is, January's got her own agenda here, which isn't the same as mine.

Sex is one thing. Sharing a bed is another, and my agenda definitely doesn't include that.

CHAPTER 5

January

Mark Taylor, you are a sex god.

The words hover on my lips, limp and satisfied and sprawled out as I am on his desk, but I have the good sense to hold them back. Mark doesn't need any more fuel for his ego even if that was the best orgasm I've had in... well, ever. Seriously, the man's fingers and tongue must have been blessed by a fairy or something.

But I'm definitely not telling him that.

What, exactly, I'm going to tell him I don't know.

First I need to sit up, but my arms are still lost in bliss, the same as the rest of me. I could happily fall asleep right here on the desk, although he probably wouldn't be amused.

And he's not talking. He's simply... *staring* at me. Shit.

With a mighty effort, I force my elbows underneath myself, propping at least part of my body upright. My legs haven't yet gotten the message that we need to get moving. My skirt doesn't magically pull itself back into place, and Mark is still between my legs, so I can't tug it down without shoving him out of the way.

I'm in the worst position to have an after-orgasm talk.

Mark's expression is completely unreadable, although the bulging erection in his pants is pretty eloquent.

"Hey." If you can't say anything, *hey* will always do.

He doesn't say anything back, not even hey. His jaw works like he's trying to decide something. Or he's grappling with a dilemma. I can't tell what's going on behind his green eyes, and it freaks me out. The man just gave me the most incredible climax—I need to see how he's feeling here.

But Mark's giving me nothing, at least nothing emotional, and maybe that's the point. Maybe this was all to put me in my place, on his desk, under his control.

Fine. I get it.

"Look." I gesture toward the door. "It's been great"—I give that a tart twist—"but I'll be going."

Lombard Street is only a few blocks away, with cabs and several Muni lines. It's not so late—or early—that my party dress will look like a walk of shame.

"No."

Finally the man speaks. His expression doesn't crack, but... but maybe there's some vulnerability in that one syllable. Maybe.

I raise an eyebrow and wait.

His eyes darken, and with infinite care, he slides his hand into my hair, lifting me toward him. When his mouth meets mine, everything tightens. His hand, his thighs next to mine, and all of me.

He's not careful now. The way he devours me, his tongue thrusting in my mouth, his chest hard against my aching breasts, his erection pressed against my still-pulsing pussy, is way too wild to be careful. Sex isn't careful or easy or *nice*, and this kiss of his is pure sex. I had the most amazing orgasm not five minutes ago, and he's already pushing me toward another one.

Two world-record orgasms and all without taking off my

clothes? Yeah, his sex-god status is pretty much confirmed now.

I hook one leg around his hips, pulling him closer. As hot as this kiss is, I want more. I want that cock of his deep inside me, and I'm not ashamed to let him know it. I feel like I can be as hungry as I want with him.

When the tip of my heel catches in his waistband and scratches the skin beneath, he moans. Oh, he likes that. His moan makes me that much more frantic, more needy.

My body becomes incoherent with desire. My hands pull at his shirt, his pants. My tongue blindly meets his thrust for thrust. My hips seek the anchor of his even as my pussy clenches emptily.

But Mark is a master cryptologist when it comes to this. With a rough jerk, he unzips his fly, his knuckles digging into my inner thigh. Now it's my turn to moan.

Some last-minute warning sputters through my brain— *Condom, you idiot, condom!*—but Mark the sex god is on it. He pulls a foil pouch from his pocket and rolls the condom on with fierce impatience. He's handling his cock likes he's so worked up he's angry, his strokes curt and forceful.

I never thought I'd be turned on by Mark touching himself like this, but it's so goddamn hot I go dizzy. Which is also a first for me during sex.

He grabs one of my hips, his fingers biting me through my dress, then hooks my other knee high on his waist. I'm open, vulnerable, utterly at his mercy, and my pussy quivers at the cool air pouring over it.

Then he slams forward and there's nothing but heat. He's not careful, he's not controlled, and *it's fucking wonderful.* I flex my knee, the better to meet every pump of his hips. We're practically rutting here, grinding out God knows how many years of sexual frustration between us.

In only a few seconds, my skin blooms with sweat. It

drips down my back, between my breasts, reminding of how animalistic this all is. He's sweating too, and in the open vee of his shirt, I see one drop travel all the way from the base of his throat to meander through the hair down below before disappearing completely.

Lucky droplet. My tongue tingles with the need to follow its path, catch it before it hits his happy trail.

I can't though, not with the mad rhythm we've set between us. I can only concentrate on holding on. My orgasm comes on like a supernova, annihilating everything in its path but creating new and wondrous sensations in the chaos left behind.

His climax grips his whole body, every muscle shuddering as his cock jerks against the rhythmic clenching of my own orgasm. His expression becomes... beautiful isn't the right word, but it touches my heart as if it were.

We both fall onto the desk, me backward and him forward. My head hits with a bang I wasn't expecting, my knees are at a weird, dangly angle, and my back wasn't meant to bend like this. But with Mark above me, panting like he's just run up California Street at a dead sprint, it's almost comfortable. He's not any more in control of this moment than I am.

I want to reach up and push back his hair, to put some tenderness into this moment, because it feels like there's too much in my heart. I have to give him some.

But that's a mistake. He pushes himself up before I can make it.

He doesn't look at me at first, wiping his brow instead. He zips up his pants, adjusts his shirt. Only then does he meet my eyes.

Maybe there's some tenderness in his gaze. Maybe. Or maybe I'm only wishing for it.

Which would be really stupid of me.

He runs one thumb along my cheekbone, and when he pulls away, the pad is black with mascara. Great. My makeup is melting, I'm covered in sweat, and my dress is hiked around my waist. Yet I still feel amazing.

With a tiny smile, he tugs down my dress and helps me off the desk. He still hasn't said anything, but maybe that's for the best. I don't know what I want to say to him either.

He takes my hand and leads me to the door. "That was… You are amazing." He brushes his lips over mine, and there's definite tenderness there.

Or is it gratitude? My mind and emotions are messy, raw. I need to get a handle on them before I do something stupid and forget this isn't about affection. Mark doesn't want it, and I can't afford it.

"Thanks." Only the word is as vulnerable as I can't be.

"You'll stay here tonight." He doesn't even offer me a choice, but I'm so worn out—the party, the ride back, the intense desk sex—I'm grateful for it. Even the thirty-minute ride across the park would be agony right now.

So I let him lead me away.

CHAPTER 6

When I wake up the next morning, Mark is already gone.

He put me in the guest room last night, giving me a kiss that started out gentle and flared into something sizzling before he gentled it again. Then he left me alone with a huge, fluffy bed. I was so tired I was only a little miffed.

I am, however, put out that he's gone before I even woke up, but there's a breakfast plate and some coffee from the café down the street—on actual china instead of a paper plate —waiting for me in the kitchen and some clothes in my exact size waiting in my bedroom. There's even underwear and a bra. Again in my exact size. I don't ponder how he knows that—instead, I want to savor this luxury completely stress-free.

There's a note with the clothes too, on heavy ivory paper and in a thick, slashing hand: *Last night was gorgeous. You were gorgeous. I'll see you soon. M.*

You were gorgeous is double underlined, and I feel each of those marks like a caress against my cheek, my jaw. Phantoms of the same hands that wrote the note.

I wonder what he means by soon. Tonight? Next week? Never?

Never seems unlikely, given the clothes and the note, but he did have me sleep in a guest bedroom rather than with him. But maybe he snores like a tank.

That makes me giggle, because Mark Taylor certainly wouldn't snore, much less like a tank. Which leaves the knotty question of why exactly he did have me sleep in here, but I'll leave that for later. I've got to get to work.

I shake out the clothes—a silk tank in peacock blue and a cream linen pencil skirt with a cashmere cardigan and adorable chunky-heeled, electric-green Mary Janes—then I poke my head in the bathroom. There's a ton of bath products there, along with lotions and creams and makeup, all unopened. Does he keep these things here for every woman he entertains? Or is this solely for me?

The fact that the clothes are exactly my size and style say it's only for me. He must have done some magic to get this here before I woke up. Or else he was so damn confident I'd go home with him he did it the day before.

Both prospects excite me. Competence or confidence—either is dead sexy in a man.

I put myself together with all the lovely things he's left me, enjoy the breakfast and coffee, then walk out to catch the Muni to work.

Only, there's already a sleek black Tesla waiting at the curb with a driver at the passenger door.

"Miss." He swings open the door. "I'm to take you wherever you want to go."

A girl could really get used to this.

When I walk into our space in the incubator—we're sharing a floor of a building in SoMa with three other start-ups—Doc immediately notices my clothes.

"Where the hell did you get those?" My right-hand woman sneers but not at me. "You look like you just came from the Marina."

"I did," I say lightly.

"Oh God." She grabs my arm. "Please tell me you're not seeing some douche from there."

In Doc's mind, the Marina is the epicenter of everything uncool and commodified about SF. Frat dudes, ladies who lunch, trust fund babies—those are the typical Marina people, and I have to say she's not wrong. Except Doc is ultracool, probably too cool for this world. She actually moved out of the City and across the bay to Oakland, which is so cool it's not even popular yet. She also has a PhD in computer science, hence the name Doc.

"Um, I wouldn't call it seeing him—"

"She left the party last night with Mark Taylor," Hallie pipes up. She's at her terminal, washing everything down with antiseptic wipes. Hallie's a bit of a germophobe, but given her horrible allergies, it's kind of understandable.

"How do you know that?" I don't bother to deny it.

"*TidBytes*." She names the premier gossip blog in the tech world. She turns her monitor to me, showing a lovely, full-screen picture of me in my supertight dress leaning into Mark like I'm about to lick him.

Had that much of my cleavage really been visible? It hadn't looked like that in the mirror when I'd left the house.

"Great," I mutter.

"It's fine." Doc firmly turns the monitor back, earning a glare from Hallie. "Did you get the funding? We've got like a week of runway left, max. Our server bill is fucking insane this month."

"I..."

Did I get the funding? Somehow Mark and I never really got around to that.

For all the grief I gave him about thinking with his dick, I certainly haven't done much better. Maybe between one of those orgasms I should have brought it up.

"Crap," Hallie whispers when she sees my expression. "But there's still Five Mile Ventures, right?"

Five Mile is Julian's firm. And no, I don't think we're on there either.

"I'm still working on it," I say, firm and upbeat and very *once more unto the breach*. "I've got it handled. Is Valentina here?"

"Hmm?" From behind her workstation, Valentina lifts her head and blinks, waking up from a catnap. She came to me with some impressive architecture knowledge, which is why I hired her on the spot.

She spent her first day sleeping at her desk, her head propped on her hand. She did it the next day too. On the third day, I was ready to fire her... and then she handed me her assignment, beautifully coded and commented and way beyond what I'd asked for.

I had no idea how she accomplished anything with her eyes always closed, but I wasn't about to question her results.

"We're testing your algorithm today," I say. "That's first priority on the server."

"Sure," she says, then closes her eyes again.

I've got four other employees. Nadia is at her desk, muttering to herself "No stinking comments in any line of this code, how the hell am I supposed to test this without any comments, what the hell are they teaching these kids in school," but Imogen, Sylvie, and Meryem won't be in until about eleven or so. Since they probably left at three this morning, I'm fine with that.

"How's the stack looking for today?" I ask Doc.

"Great. We're ticking along. We just need to fatten up the bank account."

I nod. "I know. I know."

I've got to save this company, somehow save Grace, and oh, make sure I don't tank my own future too.

"So the clothes came from Mark then?"

I should have known Doc wouldn't let it slide. "You don't like them?"

Doc dresses like a punk librarian with midlength skirts, graphic T-shirts that are too cool for me to decipher, all pulled together with men's loafers. On anyone else it would look like a mess, but Doc makes it look completely natural and utterly chic.

"Oh, it's definitely your style," she says. "But the labels are a bit... upmarket."

She doesn't say it meanly, and she's right—these clothes are definitely out of my budget.

"I stayed the night at his place." I shrug as if we might have spent all night discussing business. "He lent them to me this morning."

Doc snorts. "What, he's going to want them back? And didn't you guys have bad blood in college?"

"What? No." I've never discussed what happened with Mark with anyone, so I don't know where she got that.

"You just get this look on your face when he comes up." She scrunches up her nose like she's smelled something dead in the office fridge.

"I... I don't look like that." At least I hope I don't.

"Okay, if you say so." Doc grabs her laptop and heads for an empty desk near the whiteboard. "I've got some debugging to do."

And I've got some begging to do. First thing: call Mark and see what's what.

But when I get to my office—really it's a cubicle, but I'm the only one who has one—my resolve fails. Last night was so amazing... and now I have to act like it didn't happen when I call him.

To psych myself up, I click on my shared files, the ones that I've encrypted with my own program, the files that only my closest friends have access to. I quickly navigate to the folder where Grace's message still sits.

I first met Grace when she was looking for a roommate. We were both new to the City. She was coming from China, I was coming from South Bay. But we were both fresh meat in the SF rental market.

A man was advertising for two roommates, and I reluctantly answered. I wasn't super thrilled about living with a man I didn't know, but it beat living out of my car, which was what I'd be doing if I didn't find a room and soon. Grace was in the same situation and showed up at the apartment at the same time I did.

John, the man, turned out to be cool, and Grace became my close friend. For once, I finally had a friend who loved crosswords as much as I did, and we got hooked on *Futurama* together. We talked about almost anything. Except she never could talk about what she did.

Everyone in the valley has signed some kind of nondisclosure agreement. It's almost as common as signing a credit card slip. Only her reluctance to talk seemed to go beyond that. Like she was frightened of more than legal trouble.

Corvus, Arne Fuchs's company, had sponsored her visa, so I figured she was only afraid of losing her job and being sent back. That's one of the dirty little secrets in the valley. CEOs complain that there aren't enough American tech workers and they simply *have to* hire from overseas, but in reality, workers who depend on the company for their very right to remain in the country are the perfect drones. They'll do anything to keep their jobs.

So yeah, I figured that Corvus was maybe more secretive than most tech companies but not anything crazy. Then Grace announced that she was moving into company housing. And that she'd have a company phone from then on.

Once she was gone, her phone went dead and her email

went silent. It was like Corvus had swallowed her up. I was so terrified for her, but what could I tell the police? *She's working on some NSA-funded project and has gone dark? Oh, and she's not a citizen?*

About two months after she disappeared, I found out what she was really afraid of. Because she sent it to me herself, in an innocuously named folder on my secure shared drive. I knew it was from her because it was named after one of our favorite jokes in *Futurama*.

I have no idea how she got it to me, but she risked a lot to do it.

With two clicks of my mouse on the folder named Mom's Robots, the files fill my screen. I take in again all the information she's risking her job and her residency to give to me. All of Fuchs's plans to activate his spy network.

There are programs and algorithms and memos, probably everything that Grace dared get her hands on. All of it is shocking, but the most informative bit is a master plan written by Fuchs himself. I don't know who the audience is intended to be—his employees, his investors, or maybe simply himself—but he's giving everything away here. Like some Bond villain monologueing.

He's installed his software in every single social media app I can think of, software that will let him turn on cameras, microphones, and even the GPS. Once he flips a switch, he can watch you, listen to you, even follow you, all without your ever knowing. And it's all at least nominally legal, given the fine print he's inserted in the user agreements for all the social media sites. The fine print that no one bothers to read.

According to his memo, the program isn't active—yet. He's waiting to find just the right buyer, some government or company with deep enough pockets to afford information on every single American. I'm not sure how he's gotten the agreement from the social media sites to do this. Perhaps he offered them a cut of the rewards. Perhaps they don't know what his spyware really does. He might have claimed it was something to help target ads; who knows.

The point is, the genie is definitely out of the bottle and is just waiting for Fuchs to make his wishes.

I get chills looking over it again even though I've almost memorized it. The day after the files arrived, I started working on Ultra. I'd always loved encryption, but it became an obsession. I coded every second I could, pulled together the best team I could, and went hard after whatever funding I could.

It was all because I couldn't get to Grace since I still had no idea where she was. I can't erase his program from every phone in the world, and I can't stop him from spying on everyone—and I can't rescue Grace—but I can at least scramble whatever information Fuchs is stealing. Scramble it so badly he can never use it.

I have to do this for Grace, because she's done the riskiest thing of all—she's sent me the source code for Fuchs's spyware. That was most definitely illegal but was my entire key to blocking him. When you're fighting a giant, you need every bit of help you can get.

You also need to work your ass off, which is why I've opened the source code yet again. I've been over it and over it and over it, but I go through it for what must be the thousandth time. I'm looking for just one more weakness, one more crack, one more place to get a hold in order to pull it apart.

I'm also looking for some clue as to where Grace is. Code is filled with what we call comments: special lines that don't tell the computer what to do but explain to another programmer what the code is *supposed* to do. Comments are sort of the user manual for programmers, but they're also places for code monkeys to play and make jokes. And maybe leave a clue as to where you are and how you're doing.

Fuchs's company is located in what's known as an SCIF: Sensitive Compartmented Information Facility. No signals come in, and no signals go out. I've never met anyone who's actually been inside, but according to the rumors, cell phones are completely dead there. There's no wireless whatsoever. It's a tomb for electronics.

There are other rumors floating around too, about the draconian nondisclosure agreements employees have signed, about how they're forced to live in company dorms with everything provided so they can never leave, and about how the company tracks them twenty-four seven.

It's all terrifying and creepy, but Fuchs's incredibly rich, incredibly secretive, and those people desperately need those jobs. So even if it is true, what's anybody going to do?

Nothing.

Well, *I'm* trying. I pick up my cell phone, looking over my cubicle wall at my team humming along.

Except before I can even hit Call, Mark beats me to the punch by walking in. Totally unexpected and unannounced.

The air swells, pressing against the windows, then sucks back in with a whoosh, gathering around him. At least it seems that way, with everything pulsing like Superman himself has landed.

"Mark." I stride over and hold out my hand like we're old friends, although my knees are already weak. He's in his usual T-shirt and jeans, but has any man ever filled them out so well?

He takes my hand and pulls me close. "You look amazing," he says into my ear. "Are you wearing the underwear too?"

This is completely inappropriate for a business setting. I blush like a teenager anyway. "Let's keep this professional." I don't pull away though.

He winks at me, more dangerous than amused, a lion agreeing to play with a kitten. "Sure thing."

"What can I help you with?" I ask, loud enough for everyone to hear. I can't figure out why he's come here instead of summoning me to Sand Hill Road. Men like him don't run errands.

"I like to keep a close eye on my investments." Sure enough, he's looking around our office, taking in the workstations and whiteboards and general clutter that comes from people working long hours in a crammed space. I can't tell what he thinks of it; he's too good at shuttering his expression.

"You're funding us?" I ask with an undignified squeak. There should be more meetings, a grilling in front of all the partners at Bastard Capital, contracts, reams and hours of paperwork before we hit this point.

Doc doesn't wait for him to answer before whooping with joy. "Hot damn, we can make the server bill this month."

Mark smiles. "I like you."

"If you're going to be paying my salary, I like you too."

"Wait." I hold up my hands before this can go any further. What the hell is happening here? "Nothing's been agreed to. I haven't signed anything."

"We'll take care of that soon." He says that as if giving a start-up millions is no big deal.

Well, it probably isn't for him.

"You never said yes." I don't know why I'm pressing him when he's as good as said yes. Maybe because I can't quite believe it. Maybe because I'm looking for the catch—the clothes, the night at his place, now the funding? There has to be a catch. Mark isn't giving that away for free. Not to me.

"Are you saying no?"

Doc actually gasps at his question.

"You know I can't." I'm entirely at his mercy, in the best and worst ways.

"You always have a choice." He says that with laser precise intensity, reminding me that I do. Just as I had a choice last night. I can say no and he'll be gone, quick as that.

Except I don't want him to leave. And it's not only about the money.

"Well, I'd better say yes, or Doc will never speak to me again." I make it a joke because I'm feeling a little too raw right now, at least for a professional setting.

"You're damn right," Doc says.

"Excellent." Mark holds out his hand. "Welcome to Bastard Capital."

CHAPTER 7

Showing up at her office was meant to push January off her game, to unsettle her, but I'm the one who's on edge here.

She's in the clothes I bought for her, glasses perched on her cute nose, one pen in her hand and another pushed through her bun, scrolling through her laptop as we go through her latest data. She's completely, utterly focused, while I'm completely, utterly distracted by the way she smells, how her hair glimmers in the light, the way her top clings to her breasts.

If I'm being completely honest, I didn't only show up here because I wanted to unsettle her—I couldn't stop thinking about her.

Last night didn't get her out of my system—no way, no how—but it should have settled me down some. I'm uncomfortably close to thinking with my dick here, given how badly I want to kiss her and bend her over *her* desk.

We're definitely going to play on my desk again though. Not tonight—I've got so many fantasies about her there's no rush on repeats—but soon.

She's thinking of it too, no matter how engaged she is in her data. When she catches my eye or glances at my thigh or arm, her breath stutters in this glorious way. It's like I'm tripping up the rhythm of her lungs. I can't wait to have her panting again.

This isn't the place for it though. And really, it's fun to simply watch her. Here, she's in her element in a way I remember from college, animated and alive, pointing out her successes and failures with equal enthusiasm.

It hurt to see that enthusiasm up close and personal after she turned me down, so I stopped looking at her directly in college. She lived only in my peripheral vision until we graduated. But looking at her straight on in this moment, when her love for what she does shines so brightly, I want to capture some of that light for myself.

"Do you still do puzzles?"

She blinks as I interrupt her flow. "Um, yes." Her fingers are graceful as they set her pen down, the nails a delicate pink. It makes me think of other beautifully pink places on her. "Not crosswords—they got too easy for me. But there's all sorts of stuff online: cryptology challenges and stuff."

That gets her going too, almost as much as talking about her encryption algorithm did.

"Cryptology challenges?"

"Yeah." She shimmies in her seat, which makes her breasts shift invitingly. I shift too. "There's this one group I'm in, a women's-only group, where once a month one of us has to come up with an encrypted code the others have to solve. We call ourselves the Bletchley group."

"Bletchley?" I've never heard that name before. Is he some kind of obscure computer guy?

For a moment I think she might grab my arm. She's practically glittering with excitement. "It's a place, not a he. Bletchley is where the World War II code breakers worked. The Germans had a very sophisticated encryption system known as Enigma, and the code breakers at Bletchley worked on cracking it. Some of the first digital computers were built to help."

"Really?" In college, January had been full of amazing facts like that, much more interested in the history and arcane niches of computing than the rest of us were. I realize I haven't seen anyone so excited by pure computing like this in forever. It's all about money and branding and killer apps. Yeah, we talk big about disruption, but most of the time it's just that: talk.

She nods. "My cryptology group already has the name Bletchley, so I figured Ultra was a good enough name for an encryption company."

"Ultra?" I don't see the connection.

"Ultra was the code name given to all the information they decrypted from the German signals. We're encrypting data here, but we're also on the side of good." She shrugs, but her eyes are glinting with suppressed enthusiasm. "So... Ultra."

"It's an awesome name. How did the Enigma machine work?"

I already know she's got the plans memorized and could give a college course on it. That's the way she is. Or at least used to be.

I forgot how much I loved that about her in college.

"Oh, so it's a mechanical computer really." With a few quick keystrokes, she pulls up a schematic. "So the basic premise is a substitution cipher. *A* equals *Z*, *B* equals *Y*, and so on. Which is ridiculously easy to break."

"Even I could do that."

She smiles at me, and my heart tries to crack. I don't let it.

Whatever is between us can be physical—hell, it's already *intensely* physical—and it can be business, but it can't be personal. Silicon Valley is always ready to chew up and spit out anyone dumb enough to stumble. January hasn't come to me because she's changed her mind about turning me down in college. She's knocked on my door for money, and she's glowing like because of cryptology, not me.

The reminder makes my blood cool.

She doesn't sense the change in my temperature. "But the Enigma machine was special because it used a series of rotors to randomize the substitution. So you're typing out your message." She raises her fingers like she's about to type. "*A* equals *Z* for your first key press. But then you do another and the rotors turn, changing the substitution. So now *A* equals *Y* instead. And so on, with the cipher changing randomly with every keystroke. Which makes the code almost impossible to break."

"But the people at Bletchley did it."

She could do it, I bet. She's always been wicked smart. I can at least admire her brains along with her body.

"It was a pretty big effort. There were spies and mathematicians and engineers all involved."

She knows every one of them. I can tell by everything swirling behind her eyes. And even though I'm here solely for professional reasons—I wasn't joking about keeping a close eye on my investments—I want to hear her tell the whole story.

Something pulses between us, something new yet also carrying a whiff of memories.

This isn't supposed to be happening. Yes, I brought her back to my place last night, which I usually never do, but it was only because she was frightened. I prefer to meet women in hotels. I tell them it's because I wake up early—which is true—but that's not why. It's because I don't want just anyone in my space. And I don't want to be the bad guy when I have to escort a woman out the next morning.

In a hotel, I can leave them with room service, whatever treatment they want from the spa, and a car whenever they're ready to leave the cocoon of the room. And they can enjoy all my gifts without my having to be there.

Yes, that makes me an asshole, but one that buys his companions thousand-dollar spa days.

I didn't offer January that, but I did bring her into my home. I let her spend the night. She doesn't realize it, but even that much is more than I've given any woman before.

I want her to think it's just about sex and business, because that's what it should be. What it will be once I get myself locked down again.

"So what about *your* Ultra?" I ask. "You're programming this intense encryption algorithm, you name it after Nazi fighters—isn't that paranoid? Are 'zee Germans' coming for us?"

The moment dissolves under her embarrassment and anger. Her face floods with color, and I feel like a complete dick. But I don't apologize, because I still can't see why normal people might need the fallout shelter equivalent of encryption on their phones.

"Maybe," she says stiffly. "But with cameras and microphones and entire lives on phones, shouldn't people have the option to use the most secure software?"

"You think the phone will turn on the camera all by itself?" I mean, of course it could do that, and I've heard stories of people putting tape over their laptop cameras, but that's tinfoil-hat territory.

Judging by the look on her face—wide eyes, suddenly white cheeks—she doesn't think it's crazy at all.

"Why not?" That's only just above a whisper.

My forehead goes tight and my jaw tingles. What the hell is going on here? Is she only paranoid—or does she know something I don't?

But before I can reply, there's a knock at her cubicle door. Or rather, the wall since it doesn't have a door. Everyone else is at desks scattered through an open floor plan, and the sole perk January's given herself is this shitty, doorless cubicle. I'm going to have to do something about her lack of an office. In fact, I spent this morning before I came here finding the perfect place for the company to move.

"Someone's here with lunch?" Doc looks very puzzled as she pokes her head in. "But none of us ordered anything."

I check my smartwatch. Perfect—they're here exactly when I wanted them to be, down to the minute. "I ordered it." At January's expression, I add, "Providing food for your employees increases productivity by thirteen percent."

"I feel more productive already." With a grin, Doc goes to let the delivery company in.

January's giving me a look, half-skeptical, half-amused. "You made that statistic up."

I gesture for her to go first. "You don't know that."

"Yes I do." She snags her cardigan and covers those luscious shoulders. "You were always doing that at Stanford, making up ridiculous statistics. Like… forty-two percent of alligators prefer human flesh to chicken when given the choice."

I can't believe she remembers that. Or that the memories are amusing to her. If that tiny detail of mine has stuck with her all these years…

Why did she turn me down in college? And why is she *really* with me now?

"Doesn't sound made up to me at all." I keep my voice steady. I can't give myself away to her. "Sounds perfectly reasonable. Did you know that ninety-five percent of alligator meat tastes exactly like chicken?"

January's still laughing as she leaves her cubicle, but when she sees the delivery people unloading lunch, she stops. In fact, everyone's watching in shocked silence.

Okay, maybe I went a little overboard. But there's no way

I'm eating stale peanut butter sandwiches and a leathery apple.

Instead, we'll be eating wild salmon served with a cauliflower purée. There's freshly baked french bread in proper baskets, and the caterers are plating salads of baby greens, cranberries, and pumpkin seeds. Spring water both with and without carbonation sits in buckets of ice, and they're also sending up a top-of-the-line coffee machine. The coffee machine will stay behind since the ancient drip system I saw here wasn't fit for man or beast and Blue Bottle is too far for quick coffee runs.

"Are you going to be with us every day?" asks Hallie. She's rubbing sanitizer on her hands, which she seems to be doing every time I look over at her. I'm amazed she hasn't rubbed her skin clean off.

In fact, the crew January has assembled here is... not quite what I was expecting. For one, it's all women. And the women themselves... One has been asleep all day, another hasn't stopped muttering to herself about everything that irritates her, and another looks old enough to be someone's mom.

In the valley, there are two things coders shouldn't be—a woman or old. January either believes in her employees deeply or she's running some kind of social experiment here. Maybe both.

Hallie has stopped rubbing her hands and is staring at me. Right.

"I've arranged for lunch to be delivered every day, yes. There's an app, and once everyone's set up their accounts, you can order whatever you like each day. I had to guess today."

I sound modest, but I'm not feeling that way at all. I can tell they're impressed, and I'm feeling pretty damn pleased with myself. Especially with the expression on January's face.

I could get used to this, her face is saying.

Some part of me that I'm not supposed to acknowledge, perhaps the too-tender corner of my heart that I should be better at hiding, the corner that keeps trying to crack, wants her to get used to it.

I tell it to shut up. Tenderness has no place in this deal.

CHAPTER 8

January

Mark has been here all day, a full eleven hours, and even though I know he's running on less sleep than I am, he still looks as fresh as if he'd just woken up.

We've been going over everything related to the company —financials, programs in beta, testing benchmarks, and our targets for the future—and while I've enjoyed it, I have to admit I'm starting to wilt. Lunch was almost six hours ago, and the coffee isn't cutting my hunger any longer. Or helping my brain to stay sharp. Although the machine he's installed makes the stuff the angels must drink in heaven.

Mark, though, remains whip smart and laser focused, absorbing complex, abstract issues immediately and highlighting potential problems before I'm even done explaining.

Not to brag, but it's a rare person who can keep up with me when it comes to this stuff. And here's Mark, outpacing me. It's not competitive, not at all—and it's a relief to have someone on my level finally. At least besides my employees.

So even though I'm dead on my feet, I keep pulling up one more spreadsheet, one more source code file. Because when I grab my jacket and bag and say good night, today will be over. I won't see him again until tomorrow. At least I think not—he hasn't said anything about tonight, although he promised to in his note.

I'm already addicted to his company.

I'm going through the code Meryem gave me yesterday when I suddenly come to with his voice in my ear, whispering my name.

"January." His hand's on my shoulder, and his fingers are brushing my cheek. He's trying to wake me up, but I don't want to. Not when this dream of him is so nice.

"I've called the car. We're going home."

That makes me sit up. *Home?* Does he mean his place? We haven't discussed anything at all, and I at least need to run by my apartment to water my orchids and grab some fresh clothes. I can't keep wearing gifts from him. Even if I'd love to see what he picks out for me next.

"Okay." I shake my head to chase off my drowsiness. "Let me check NextBus and see when the N Judah is coming—"

"Don't argue." He's not mean about it, just commanding. Commanding and sexy. "The car's out front now. Are you hungry, or do you want to go straight home?"

There's that word again, as if his home is my home. Or maybe my place isn't nice enough for him to ever consider it a home. Compared to his house, anything else would be a shack.

My stomach rumbles, answering for me. Okay, so I can't lie and say I'm not hungry, but I also don't want to fall asleep in the middle of some fancy restaurant.

"I could eat." I barely get that out before I'm attacked by a massive yawn.

"We'll stop by my club then. We'll get a private room."

I can't tell if he's teasing or not.

When we pull up to his club, a building that's remarkably discreet considering how ornate it is, I figure he's probably teasing. This is not a place where you can sleep as you eat.

This is a place where the richest of the rich come to socialize and grow even richer with the backroom deals they make here.

For a moment I wonder if Fuchs will be here, if I'll have to see him again. The thought climbs up my spine, locks my joints, even as I try to keep stumbling forward.

Mark hooks his arm around my waist, taking my weight as if it were no more than a feather. His cheek brushes mine as he leans in close. "You okay?"

I nod. "Just tired."

"We can leave."

I want to, but I can't hide like a rabbit all the time. "No, I'll be okay."

I feel Mark's jaw tightening, the muscle and bone hard against my cheek. He isn't quite buying it, but he leads us forward anyway.

A uniformed doorman whisks us inside with easy deference. Before I know it, he's taken our coats and my bag and told us that the wild mushroom pappardelle is particularly excellent today.

"I'll be using my usual room," Mark says.

The doorman accepts that with a nod, and we move forward through double french doors into the main area.

Holy heck. My mouth wants to drop open, but I don't let it. This... this is pretty overwhelming though. The carpet looks like it came straight from Turkey, the chairs are all burgundy leather, and the place is covered with gleaming wood accents. Even the ceiling gleams since it's covered with copper tiles. There's a double-sided fireplace in the middle of the room and a baby grand tucked into a corner where a pianist plays an accompaniment to the low conversations taking place at the tables.

I'm so engrossed in taking everything in I almost miss Mark's stumble.

I freeze. Fuchs must be here. He must have followed me, first to the party, then here...

But as I scan the room for him and don't see him, some of my cold fear leaves me. Why would Mark be afraid to see Fuchs? He has no idea what the man has planned.

So something—or someone—else must be spooking him.

My gaze falls on Julian then, and I instantly see why Mark's upset. Julian's at a table with a woman so beautiful it's like she's stepped out of a magazine. But there's nothing airbrushed about her high cheekbones, wide-set eyes, and flawlessly painted mouth. Or the body under her designer clothes.

I dress really well for a programmer and take pride in being put together, but I'm nothing compared to this woman.

Mark can't take his eyes off her either, but he's not happy about it. His jaw keeps twitching, like he's holding back an eruption.

"Who is she?" I whisper.

"Callie," he says in more of a growl than a whisper. "Logan's wife. She has some fucking nerve."

Mark's obvious distress gets to me. I want to be on his side, to stand with him.

We're not allies though, not really. I need to remember that.

"What happened?"

I want to hear a tale of how Logan cheated—he strikes me as the type, with his too-good looks—how Callie was right to go to Julian. After all, she's a free woman, the same as the rest of us. She doesn't owe Logan anything.

"Nobody knows," he says. "I know what it looks like with Logan, but he really did love her. *Does.*" Mark shakes his head, his dark hair falling over his brow. "Logan thought everything was great. And then one day she was gone. Without a trace. Julian came to us and said any messages to

Callie could be sent through him. Like Logan was going to track her down and do something to her."

Mark is furious, but he's holding it in so tightly he's vibrating. Strangely, I'm not a bit afraid. Maybe because he's pissed on behalf of his friend.

A detail floats back to me. "You said wife, not ex-wife."

That seems like an important distinction, one Mark wouldn't slip up on.

"She never started divorce proceedings. And Logan's so fucked up over her leaving, he'll never do it."

I take another look at Callie, peering past the blinding perfection. Her eyes are tight, her skin too pale, her mouth held rigid. She's not easy, not at all.

She looks as broken up as Mark says Logan is.

Mark grabs my hand, making me jump. Oh no. He can't—

But he is, pulling me in his wake as he heads for them. I pull back, not hard, but to try to slow him down, get him to rethink this.

He doesn't though, and as we get close, I hear Callie saying, "I need to do something, Julian! I can't go on like this. Why hasn't he called a lawyer—"

She stops dead then because Julian is rising, a nasty smile on his face as he stares down Mark. When she sees who's coming, her face goes whiter than fog. She turns her head away, but not before I see her rapidly blinking as if her eyes are burning.

"Funny seeing you here," Julian drawls.

Awesome. They're going to have another showdown. At least pictures of this won't make the front page of *TidBytes* since it's a private club. The story will though.

"Not so funny," Mark says, "considering I'm a member of this club. Along with Logan." He sends that to Callie.

She whips her head around, her too-pale skin suddenly going red. She looks like she might be choking. "Is he here?"

Mark snorts. "Why? Can't stand the thought of facing him?"

She rises, her movements jerky. "I knew this was a bad idea."

Sympathy for her pokes at my sternum. Mark seems convinced she's the bad guy, but her obvious distress convinces me otherwise.

"Leaving so soon?" Mark asks. "But we haven't caught up."

She doesn't even look at him as she shoves away her chair. "Tell Logan I'm getting a lawyer. Tell him he needs one too."

"Tell him yourself," Mark says, but she leaves without another word.

I'm shaking with anxiety and embarrassment, the tension of the scene sinking into me. Now that Callie's gone and the Bastards aren't here, there's no one to stop these two except me. I'm not sure if I have that kind of influence over Mark—probably not—and I definitely don't have it over Julian.

There goes my nice, relaxing dinner.

"She needs to talk to him," Mark says in a tone that doesn't carry past the three of us. "She can't leave him without a word. Even you have to see that."

Julian shakes his head. "Just leave her alone. She doesn't owe you anything."

"And Logan?"

Julian doesn't bother to answer. He's looking at me now, and his smile softens but remains mocking. "I see you've found a VC backer," he says. Not mean but more like he's sad for me. That he can see a bad end here.

"Yes, she did." The triumph in Mark's voice is ugly. "And if I catch you—"

I pull my hand out of his and take two steps away. "Catch him doing what? And *you'll* do what?"

The money, Grace, Chloe—all those things flash through my mind as I confront him. Are we only things to him and his friends, toys to buy and discard as their whims take them?

Suddenly I feel nothing but sympathy for Callie.

"Well, it looks like she won't knuckle under. Good for her."

I hate Julian right now too, so I don't acknowledge his comment. This is between me and Mark, and Julian can keep his smarmy ass out of it.

Mark's expression never softens an inch. I wonder if the entire place is staring at us, but I don't want to look and confirm it. Better to pretend that they're not.

Mark takes my elbow this time, firm enough to let me know that I really should not make a scene.

Oh, I won't. I'll wait until we're alone for that.

"Julian, fuck off," he says.

Julian's laughter follows us as we go down a hall. Or rather, as Mark marches me down the hall, my elbow still in his hand. I don't fight, but I also don't try to keep up. I'm not afraid, because while he's angry—potently so—he's controlling it.

And I'm angry too, that he could pull that stunt in front of Julian.

He draws me into a room off the hall and shuts the door behind him.

Turns out he wasn't joking about the private rooms—this one is done up like an old-fashioned library with rows and rows of leather-bound books, high-backed chairs, and even a roaring fire. With the nighttime fog pressing against the windows, shielding the bay from view, the fire is luxuriously warm.

There's a table with two chairs in the center of the room,

set with snow-white linen and china, gleaming silver and crystal. It's like a dream I never want to wake up from.

Except, of course, for the very angry male standing across the doorway. I keep my eyes on the fog outside the window. Cold and damp and obscuring as it is, it's still safer than looking into Mark's green eyes.

"I'm not your possession," I say, quiet but steely. "Taking your funding, sleeping with you... that doesn't mean you own me."

The Mark I used to know would have immediately apologized. This Mark doesn't.

"It doesn't mean I own you. But it does mean something."

"Not that you can play some kind of caveman game over me with Julian. Especially not in front of everyone."

Twice now, I don't add. The first time seemed to be mostly about Julian and Logan. This time... this time it feels more about me. My pulse tingles in my veins.

"I shouldn't have done that," he says finally. It's not quite an apology, but at this point I'm not sure I'm going to get one. And I'm not sure if I'm going to walk out of here if I don't.

I tell myself I'm unsure because I can't afford to make him mad, that I need his help with Ultra. But that's not the whole truth—my uncertainty includes my new feelings for him. Yes, he can be a real asshole... but the glimpses I see of the man beyond that are so enticing. So compelling.

"Please don't do it again." I wrap my arms around myself but don't turn to face him. I'm not sure if I'm ready for that yet.

His sigh fills the space between us. "Logan was shattered when Callie left. Still is. When you see your friend hurting like that and can't understand why, when you can't see what he did to deserve it, it makes you irrational. And fucking Julian, rubbing all our faces in it..."

I still don't turn, even though I do understand. Look at me, here with him, all to save my friend.

"I'm sorry," he says finally. "I was a jerk. I shouldn't have done that to you."

He's apologized. I was so unready for that it hits me right in the middle of my chest. But before I can respond or even figure out what all these emotions are rushing through me, there's a knock at the door.

In a few seconds, the room is filled with servers putting together a full meal and even a bar cart in case the champagne on ice isn't enough for us. It's amazing and ridiculous all at once. But then the scent of beef hits my nose and I'm mostly hungry. The waiter pulls off the silver domes to reveal steak frites, and I could cry with happiness.

The other waiter holds out my chair for me. "Anything to drink?" he asks in perfectly polished tones.

"Um…" I try to think of something sophisticated enough to eat with this as I sit down. My cocktail knowledge is sketchy. "A Manhattan?" I try.

"Of course."

Just as efficiently as they set everything up, they're gone again, leaving me with some amazing-looking steak and fries, a cocktail… and Mark.

I can't help myself anymore—I have to ask. "What is all this?"

The dinner, the clothes, the car, the lunch: he's pampering me, but there's an edge to it. He wants me to be impressed. But also overawed.

Which I am, but… I want the edge to dull. I want to roll around in this luxury without worrying about slicing my heart open. Which is ridiculous.

"This?" He raises an eyebrow, looking too damn good as he does. "It's my club. Maybe a little over the top, belonging to a private club, but it is nice."

"No, I mean… The clothes, the car, being at Ultra all day, and then this. What do you mean by it?"

It can't be all just for me, and if this is a mind game, it's a very weird one. Okay, there are plenty of companies that give their workers lunches, laundry service, gyms, everything they could ever need from the outside—but that's to keep them at their desks longer. This isn't about squeezing more productivity out of me.

So what is it?

He arranges his silverware, looking uncertain for the first time I can remember. At least since he asked me out the first time. "None of your other lovers ever took you out?" He finally raises his eyes, his hard composure back in place. "You must have been with some real assholes."

Lover. He's using that instead of *boyfriend* to put me in my place, to remind me that it's all physical. Or…

I shift as I realize what else it could be. He's reminding *himself.*

"I don't date tech bros," I say coolly, "so, no, they haven't been assholes."

I wait for him to say *but you're dating me,* except he doesn't fall for the obvious bait. "Would you rather we grabbed burritos from some hole-in-the-wall in the Mission?"

"No." I take a bite of steak and almost moan because it's beyond perfect. "But sometimes it's fun to do that too. Don't you have fun sometimes in your whole 'master of the universe' shtick?"

"It's not a shtick," he says shortly.

"Okay, fine. But you do have fun?"

"Sure. Last week one of our start-ups was bought by Google. That was fun."

"I mean normal-person fun." I gesture with my fork. "Something that doesn't involving making or spending scads of money."

As his face twists in confusion, it hits me suddenly. What's really different about him since college, beyond the money and power and sex-god status.

He never has fun anymore. Which is just about the saddest thing I can think of.

CHAPTER 9

Do I have fun? Normal-person fun?

I'm not struggling with January's question, not at all. It's only that "normal person" isn't even part of my vocabulary anymore.

I have fun, I'm sure I do, but... normal-person fun? Like being part of an online cryptology group?

I don't have anything like that in my life. I left mundane life a long time ago. I try to think of something that isn't work or hanging out with the Bastards that I've done recently. Something I've actually *enjoyed* too, which narrows things down considerably.

Licking your pussy as you sprawled on my desk and screamed with pleasure.

Okay, that's not what she means either, but it *was* fun.

"I can't give you a good example at the moment," I say.

She waggles a smug eyebrow. *Knew it*, that expression says.

"There's a thing about money," I say. "Something that's hard to explain."

She makes a mock sympathetic face, and I'm tempted to spank her for it. Maybe I'll spank her tonight. Make her ass nice and pink as she gasps with every stroke of my hand. No pain—I'm not into that—but enough to get a nice tingle going.

"Don't get too sassy," I warn her. I take a deep breath, wrestling with how much of myself to expose to her. How much of myself I can entrust to her.

That's the other thing that's hard to explain about money —once you have a massive amount, it's hard to tell if someone's with you for yourself... or your bank account.

I've seen Logan get burned bad with Callie. And I don't want January and I to end up in that kind of agony.

"Once we—the Bastards—got to where we are, we didn't know who we could trust. Everyone wants a piece of us: to make a pitch, find out our secrets, or plain old ask for money. Or screw us any way they can."

My jaw tightens. Like Julian. Competition is one thing, stealing Logan's wife is another.

January's gaze turns wary. Shit, I've got to stop with the Julian stuff around her.

I clear my throat. "It just got easier to stick together since we know we've got each other's backs. And when one of us stepped out and trusted another person... Well, she betrayed him with Julian."

Okay, that slipped out before I could stop it. But it's the perfect example of what I mean.

She's got her chin in her hand, watching me. I can't tell if she's feeling sympathy... or if she's only tired.

I'd rather she was tired. Honestly.

"It doesn't have to be you against the world."

So she's going with sympathy. I don't need it.

"Really? And what brought you to my door? Just your inescapable attraction to me?"

She flinches as my words land. Shit. I'm an asshole.

She's asked what all this is about, and the sad truth is I want to impress her. I want to show her how far I've come from that kid who stuttered through asking her out in college. I want her to be so deeply ensnared by me she won't even dream of saying no to me this time. And if I have to use my wealth to do it, I will.

There's no way in hell I'm letting her within a mile of that truth though.

"I guess you're right," she says with tight misery. "I'm here for the same mercenary reasons as all the rest."

Only, she isn't. There's something deeper than a founder's optimism in their start-up. Something that terrifies her, something that chases through her eyes when she thinks I'm not looking.

January sets her fork down with agonizing precision, her mouth a curve of sorrow. "I suppose I should go. Maybe I'll see you tomorrow, but you don't have to—"

"I'm sorry." I reach across the table and take her hand, which is cold. "Again. I'm supposed to be the personable one, but clearly I'm fucking up tonight."

Mark Taylor, master negotiator. At least that's who I'm supposed to be. For all my big talk about not letting her under my skin, she's already in deep. Deep enough to throw me off my game.

Who's playing who now here?

She gives me a brave smile, but the edges of it hurt. "It's been a long day."

"Longer than usual?"

She shakes her head. "No, not really. You know how it is. Anything under eighty hours a week is part-time."

"Yeah. When we were first starting out, we had rented this ancient place in East Palo Alto. Our workstations were all in the living room, and when things got crazy—and they were always crazy—we'd sleep under the table. We had sleeping bags under there and everything."

She stares at me for a long moment, so long I actually feel self-conscious. Which I haven't felt in damn near forever. I forgot how miserable that sensation felt.

Almost as miserable as when she first turned me down.

"You miss those times," she said. "Right now the way you're smiling... You used to smile like that."

It sounds like she misses that smile. And what the hell does she know about how I smile now?

"Really?"

She draws back, hides behind her glass. "Yes. We were friends back then. I remember."

No, *she'd* thought we were friends. I was infatuated with her. God, but it hurt to face her rejection, to know that she never felt anything more for me. At least it did back then.

I thought I was over it, but the way she's reeling me in makes me doubt myself. But I keep all that in. Being ruthless here is fine. Being petulant is not. It gives too much of my true feelings away.

I shrug. "College was a long time ago. Being a partner in a VC firm is pretty different from trying to pass CS115."

"Right." She sets her glass down with a sharp clink. "It was. So we're in business together and we're sleeping together. But we're not friends."

I've never wanted to be just a friend, especially not now that we've fucked. "What we have here is more complicated, don't you think?"

I keep my voice cool, the better to bring the tone of this down. I don't want to hurt her, and I don't want to lash out with my own stupid wounds. All right, so maybe I'm hiding some deeper feelings from her. But she's hiding some shit from me too.

Her own voice drops several degrees. "You're right. Speaking of that, when do I sign the paperwork? It's not that

I don't trust you"—her smile is sharp—"but I'd like to make it all legal."

"Tomorrow." I take a sip of my tequila, the better to clear the dryness from my throat. "Anjie and Elliot are drawing up the paperwork."

"Anjie?" There's the faintest pulse of jealousy there. I have to look down to hold back my surge of triumph.

"Anjelica Caprice. Our office manager. She'll be there for the signing."

"Oh." January takes a long pull on her cocktail, one that has her visibly reacting. I get the impression she doesn't deal with hard liquor often. But it's put a lovely glow in her cheeks, given the faintest hint of unfocusedness to her expression.

"Did you like it?" I gesture to her nearly empty tumbler.

"Yes." She runs a finger around the rim. "It was all so, so lovely."

And there it is, my reward for the evening. The expression from her I've been hungering for since she stepped into my firm—wistful, grateful, and oh so soft.

Pliable. That's the word to put to her. I want to wrap her around me, so tight she'll never let go.

I shove my own empty tumbler away from me. "Do you want to get out of here?"

CHAPTER 10

January

Mark's house remains just as jaw-dropping on a second visit.

We're in his living room, sipping port from the most delicate glasses, the glitter of the bay spread outside the massive picture window. Light is amplified and twisted by the water, almost as if the bay is painting with the light the city is tossing at it.

I'd suspect him of bringing me here specifically at night to be awed by this view, but having seen it in the daylight, I know it's equally impressive then.

And it looks like I'll be seeing it again come morning. What clothes will he choose for me this time? Or will I just get a voucher for one of the upscale boutiques lining Lombard Street?

The thought excites me rather than repels me. I'm not exactly selling myself here, but the money issue between us is prickly and large.

But not as all-encompassing as our attraction.

"January." Mark comes up behind me and runs a hand down my bare arm. He's taken my cardigan and my shoes. I'm all too aware of my skirt, shirt, and underwear, the only things between my bare skin and him.

After our long day, I should be exhausted. Instead, I'm almost jittery with anticipation. Having Mark this close to me, with all the erotic electricity crackling between us, is better than a shot of adrenaline.

"It's so beautiful," I say. He knows that, but the scene before us is the kind of beauty that has to be remarked on.

"I know." He lowers his head to the crook of my neck and inhales deeply. The appreciative noise he makes has my knees going weak. "So beautiful." He hooks a finger into the strap of my shirt. "Let's make it even more so."

He takes my glass, then pulls my shirt off with agonizing slowness, and if it weren't for the occasional tremble I feel in his fingers as they make contact with my skin, I'd think he was doing this just to torment me. But he's tormenting himself too, which is so, so hot. A powerful man holding back—painfully so—is my weakness, it seems.

When he finds the waistband of my skirt, I swear my skin is one sustained vibration. If I can't be naked soon, have his hands hold me, his cock impale me, I might shatter.

This time he doesn't bother with slowness. He jerks my skirt down my legs with an impatience that is as intoxicating as it is rough. I've never been wanted like this before, with a desire so potent it threatens to tip over into madness.

This is the kind of stuff the poets talk about, that heartbroken singer-songwriters wail about, and it's happening to me.

Once my skirt is gone, Mark grabs me around the waist and pulls me into him. His kiss is all demand and fire, threatening to overwhelm me. I set my hands on his jaw to steady myself and kiss him back, meeting his demands with my own need. I rub myself against him, needing friction to cool the sensations racing over my skin. But that only makes it worse, heightening my awareness of my bra cinching my breasts, my panties hiding my clit, and his whole outfit covering all of him.

"Naked," I pant against his throat. He's got the faintest hint of stubble there, enough to make the texture interesting, more than enough to drive me insane when I run my mouth over it.

"My thoughts exactly." He misunderstands and reaches for the fastening of my bra. But when his fingers find my nipples, I don't care anymore.

He didn't do this last night, and I'm suddenly grateful, because he pulls my nipples to such tight, aching points I think I might pass out. The dizziness is back, the afterwash from the vortex of pleasure swirling through me.

If he'd done this during our first time together, I would have imploded. There would have been nothing left of me but scorch marks on his desk. Thank God he hadn't or else I would have missed this.

He cups my breasts and lowers his head. When his tongue finds one of my nipples, giving it a slow, appreciative lick, my entire body pulses. The shockwaves collect in my pussy and vibrate through my clit.

"Again, please." I don't even realize I'm ready to beg him until I do.

He looks up at me from under his lashes, the green of his eyes wicked. His smile is knowing and secret all at once. "Liked that, did you?"

He rolls a nipple through his fingers, tugging gently, and I grab his head to steady myself. His hair is almost too soft, at least compared to how intense his fingers feel on me.

"Should I be coy?" I ask.

"Hell no." He licks my nipple again to punctuate that. "You're not made for coyness. You're made for full-throated pleasure."

He makes me sound so sensual, so seductive, as if I'm a

siren come to life. I've never thought of myself like that, but he makes me believe it.

"Give it to me then." I grab his head to hold him in place, his mouth now fully fastened on my breast. The pull of his lips and tongue is driving me to full on demanding. "Give me all that pleasure."

There's no answer, probably because he's moved on to my other breast, loving it with his mouth. If he keeps up with this, then I suppose that's my answer.

But of course this is Mark, and he must have the last word. "You want it then? Take off your panties." He crosses to the couch and tosses a cushion to the floor. "Kneel."

I remember what he said about the toys, about not needing them. I realize now that he was entirely serious. He's going to turn me inside out with only himself.

I don't take my eyes off him as I pull off my panties—already soaked—and kneel on the pillow. This excites him, my complete and utter focus. I can tell from the way his breathing begins to hitch, his lungs working overtime. It excites me too.

The cushion is too big for this, and I roll a bit as I find a position. Mark is there instantly, steadying me.

"Okay?"

I nod and cross my hands in front of me. "Like this."

"Don't pose," he says. "It's not like that. Just look out the windows."

Not like that? Then what is it?

I look out the windows obediently. The view is still as lovely as ever. It's the kind of thing your eyes would never grow tired of.

Mark crouches behind me then. I can't see him, but I sense his posture, hear that his knees haven't touched the floor, but his heat and power are coiled around me, almost touching me. I start to turn my head to look—

"Straight ahead." It's not a command, but he means to be obeyed. "Trust me."

That last isn't a command at all—there's softness under his steel. The softness makes me melt. I look ahead and lean back, just enough to brush against him.

His sigh is sharp with pleasure, and he wraps his arm around my waist, pulling me into him. His chest is broad, and I can feel the slabs of muscle tight against my shoulders. Before me, the bay glitters in the velvet dark.

"You feel so good." He presses his face into my hair. "And smell so good." The hand on my waist slips lower, dipping into my folds. "Here too. Here you smell best of all."

The delicious compliment washes over me, but the delight barely fades before Mark starts to explore my pussy, reacquainting himself with all the sensitive spots he found the night before.

He's one quick learner, because with only a few flicks of his fingers, I'm reduced to panting, rubbing myself against his hand as his arm anchors me at the waist.

"Look at you, fucking yourself against my hand." His words are filthy, but his tone is so warm I want to wrap myself in them. "Is this what you want? My fingers inside you, stretching you, rubbing that aching clit until you come all over my hand?"

"Yes." I'm practically sobbing, my fingernails sunk into his wrist as I hold on for dear life, pushing his hand deeper into me. "Please, please."

If I don't come, I'm going to die. People say that all the time, but I really mean it. I can't hold on to this much sensation. It's going to pull me apart at the seams.

"Hmm." His hand slows, then comes to almost a complete stop except for the lightest strokes of my clit. He's not letting me come, but he's not letting me come down either, the

monster. "I don't think that will work. You want all the pleasure, don't you?"

He thrusts against my back, his erection sliding along my
spine. I bite my lip hard, but the moan comes out anyway.

"That's what you want instead of my fingers, don't you?
My cock?" He thrusts again as he circles my clit.

My pussy clenches; I'm close to orgasming only from this
teasing.

"You know I do." I force that out through gritted teeth
because I'm done with the foreplay. I need him—and yes, his
cock—now.

Through some kind of magical strength, he has me straddling him on the floor in only a few seconds. I barely have
time to process he's even moving before my thighs are
spread, my hands braced on his shoulders, and his cock
nestled in my folds.

His naked cock. He's still fully clothed, only his pants
unfastened. Him being covered and me being nude somehow
makes me feel insanely powerful, as if I'm the goddess here
and he's the mortal I've chosen to please me.

"Condom," he grunts, and again he performs some magic,
the foil packet appearing in his hand. "So you don't worry."

"Just hurry." I rock my hips, urging him on. I could come
simply from the feel of his pants against my thighs, I'm so
wound up. But I want to come with him inside me, to wrest
free all that pleasure he promised me.

He doesn't tease me this time. In fact, he finally seems as
frantic as I am. That first thrust lifts my knees clear off the
floor and fills me so completely every inch of me throbs. The
second thrust is even wilder than the first.

I can't meet him in this frantic rhythm. I can only hold on
and chase my own orgasm, which is coming on fast enough
to have my eyes screwing closed. I can't look right now; I can
only feel.

And feel I do. My body turns inside out as I climax, everything a sustained, throbbing spark.

Mark comes with a harsh grunt, his body shuddering into mine.

When I open my eyes, the picture window is directly in front of me, the scene as serene and splendid as ever. While I was having the orgasm of a lifetime, the bay simply kept on being dazzling. I suspect Mark has positioned us exactly so, since he was so insistent I look.

We still haven't fucked in a bed.

And as he shifts under me, the fabric of his pants abrading my bared inner thighs, I realize I've never yet seen him naked.

CHAPTER 11

January

I'm in lust with Mark Taylor.

I let my head fall back against the chair as those words roll through my mind. It's three in the morning, and I can't sleep, so it's the perfect time to ponder such thoughts.

Mark is still sleeping—I think, since I'm in the guest bedroom again and he's not—so I've crept into his office with my laptop, intending to do some work. If I can't sleep, I might as well make the most of it.

Except that my laptop is closed and my mind is full of him.

Lust is an interesting word. *I'm in lust* is an even more interesting phrase. It starts out almost sounding like *I'm in love*, then it takes a hard, hissing turn at the end. It's not hearts meeting like you thought it would be; it's bodies slapping together.

Or maybe it's bodies and desires meeting. Carnal, yes, but not crude. There is no romance, but it is intensely felt.

I close my eyes and run my hands down my torso, skim them over my breasts and belly, curl them caressingly around my neck. It's not even close to Mark's touch, but I need something. I've become an addict for him after only two nights.

Outside, the neighborhood is almost eerily quiet. I thought my place in the Outer Sunset was pretty calm, but now I'm particularly aware of how often cars and people go down my street, even in the middle of the night. Nothing moves outside here, as if even the cars don't dare disturb a billionaire's rest.

I should be getting the most restful sleep I've had since I moved to the city, but I suppose now that I'm used to noise, the quiet keeps me awake.

Or maybe it's awareness of him just down the hall. Or at least I assume so. I haven't yet seen his room.

I feel a bit like Belle in *Beauty and the Beast* when she's tempted to search the forbidden wing of the castle. Mark might roar at me, but my curiosity is a powerful thing.

What's his room like? What's he hiding in there? Is he even in there? If I find his room empty, would I have the bravery to search it?

But all those questions will remain unanswered tonight. Whatever we have, it's not a relationship and it wouldn't survive my invading his privacy. I know that without having to test it.

So instead I sigh and open up my laptop. My email program tells me I have almost two hundred emails waiting for me, and my Slack channel tells me I have God knows how many messages waiting. Hopefully it's just the ladies of Ultra quoting movies at each other rather than anything serious. Sometimes—often, actually—our work communications devolve into hilarity.

I ignore all that. Work might be calling, but I want to take some time to recall why I'm doing all this.

Once more, I open the files Grace sent to me. Only this time as I review them, I'm not thinking of how to stop Fuchs.

I'm thinking of what to tell Mark. If I should trust him with this.

This is a lonely fight I've chosen. I didn't dare tell any of my team the real reason I started Ultra. Besides Grace, who is God knows where, I'm the sole holder of this massive secret.

I want to share some of this burden, but I'm not even certain if I told Mark about all this that he'd even be concerned. Or maybe he'd be concerned but wouldn't think it was his place to interfere.

Mark and Fuchs are of the same breed—masters of this particular universe. Grace and I, on the other hand, are both cogs. Mark may be sleeping with me and showering me with gifts, but that doesn't change our fundamental places in this ecosystem. Fuchs remains his natural ally.

I want Mark to be my ally though. I want someone to finally trust in all this, someone with the strength to fight Fuchs on his ground. If Mark was on my side, everything would be so much easier. Mark can talk to people I can't, twist arms that I wouldn't dare to touch. And Fuchs would be afraid of him.

Those considerations are tempting. If it were only me in danger here, they'd be enough to convince me to trust Mark.

But there's still Grace, out there somewhere, putting herself on the line to pass this to me.

Grace, where are you? Are you okay?

Of course there's no answer. I close all the files, sighing as I do. It's time to take the risk I've been trying to avoid. But Grace's been silent too long, and I need to know she's okay.

I drag a program I've been working on into the shared secure file. It's a simple messaging app, basically a stripped-down text messenger but encrypted up the wazoo. If my testing is correct—and I'm pretty sure it is—Fuchs won't be able to read the messages even if he can intercept them.

Grace herself will have to enter the code to unscramble them. I hope I've made the code obvious enough for her to figure out.

The app itself looks completely innocuous. I've disguised it as a Mandarin-English dictionary. The graphics are crude, like something thrown together for a quick buck. Not at all like a supersecret messaging system. In my head, I've been calling it "tin can on a string."

If she's caught communicating with me, she could be in big trouble. But she's already left me the files; I'll leave it up to her to decide if using the app is worth the risk. I close the shared file, praying Grace finds it soon and can install it. I don't dare leave any instructions in case she's caught accessing the secure shared file.

I close my laptop, my nerves sparking like downed power lines. I haven't done anything wrong, at least not technically, but the sense of sick guilt, like Fuchs is waiting around the corner to pounce on us, is horribly powerful.

When the light snaps on in the office, my heart leaps out of my skin.

Mark is there in the doorway, wearing only a pair of sweatpants. Holy hell, I wasn't wrong about the hours in the gym. His biceps, shoulders, and pecs are like art, and his abs... Is there something beyond art? Maybe miraculous? With the hair dusting his skin, so smooth with a hint of a tan, potency practically shimmers off him.

He looks so solid, so strong, that I want to launch myself into his arms. I want to beg him to be on my side, to help me fight this battle.

Instead, I swallow down my anxiety. It burns my throat as I do.

"You okay?" he asks. His voice is rough, his eyes heavy. He must have just woken up. It's a good look on him.

I thank God I shut the laptop already. "I couldn't sleep.

You know how sometimes you get ideas and they won't leave you alone?"

"Yeah. Except it hasn't happened to me in a while."

I lean over the desk, wishing he would come closer. "Do you still wish you were coding? Or is that too lowly for you now?"

As if hearing my secret wishes, he comes over, pulls me out of the chair, then sits down, this time with me in his lap. His skin is hot, rough with hair, and he smells... I'll forever call that particular scent "Sleepy Mark." It'll haunt my dreams after this.

"There's no point in my coding anymore." He runs his nose down my neck, teasing me with the possibility of a kiss. "I'm too rich to waste the time."

My first instinct is to tweak him, but he sounds so sad I hold back. "I would think you'd be too rich to *not* do whatever you want."

"It's a funny thing about being wealthy"—this time his lips find my skin, and I shiver even though I'm burning up—"you find that a shit ton of your time is spent managing your money or adding to it. Like a treadmill that won't stop."

I tip my head to the side, encouraging him to keep going. "You can always get off the treadmill. If you want."

I don't know why I'm pushing him like this. Being the master of the tech universe suits him. Except... there's that thread of sadness in him. It pulls at me.

"Are you trying to get me to work for you?" He's amused, but it's muted. "I don't come cheap."

Costs. Expenses. Money. That's what it always seems to come down to between us. And no, I can't afford him. This relationship will likely end up costing me more than I ever wanted it to, no matter how hard I try not to fall for him.

"You always wanted to make things in college," I say. "Do you make anything now?"

"Money."

"Yes, you do. You're very good at that."

He leans close to my ear. His breath tickles in the hottest way. "I'll tell you a secret—once you have enough money, it just starts making itself."

"Like perpetual motion?"

"Pretty much." He's found the most sensitive patch of skin between my ear and my neck, a place I didn't even know existed, and he's making that skin sing.

"I don't think I'd ever want to stop making things. Even if they'd only be for my own curiosity."

"When we sell Ultra to the highest bidder, you won't have to. You can be a woman of leisure. Travel the world."

"Maybe I'll become a VC." I say that to hide how unsatisfying the other stuff sounds. I want my friend to be free. I want the world safe from Fuchs. Traveling the world seems selfish compared to those.

Mark shakes his head. "You'd be miserable. There're no puzzles to solve, no tricky circuits to design. Only twisting people's arms over deals. And always chasing the next unicorn."

No, I wouldn't like that. And the Mark I knew in college wouldn't have either.

But he's clearly not the man he was in college. He's more confident, more powerful, more dangerous.

More attractive.

I could say no to him then, but I definitely can't now.

CHAPTER 12

I haven't slept past four a.m. in years. Even on the weekends, I'm up and working as soon as my eyes open.

In the tech world, that's a feature, not a bug. Sleep is for the weak. Insomnia is a life hack.

Occasionally I consider trying to sleep in; trying to recapture those lazy weekend mornings from college. I don't know if my body would let me. Maybe I've been the hard-driving, workaholic venture capitalist for too long now. Maybe I can never find my way back to relaxed mornings.

Before today I wouldn't have considered that a problem.

I definitely wasn't relaxed this morning when I woke up. My body knew before my mind was even operating that January was near.

Without dressing, I went to find her. The need for her was too much to resist.

With her on my lap, talking about what she'll do after her company is sold, the calm I was searching for when I woke up settles on me. She's warm and exactly the right size to nestle with me in this chair. I could keep her here forever, doing all my work while she clings to me. And when the mood takes us, I could bury myself in her. We'd never have to leave this room.

The mood is taking me now, and she's right here in my arms.

I take her chin and tilt it up, lowering my face to hers. Her eyes widen with a kind of innocent surprise that makes me hard as a rock. But when our mouths finally do meet, it's... *sweet.*

There's no other word for it. This kiss ensnares me like honey. If I tried to fight it, it would only pull me in deeper. Only, I don't want to fight it. I want to kiss her like this forever, to have the taste of January-in-the-morning on my tongue every morning.

Our lips brush again and again, our tongues meeting like shy strangers, and it sets me aflame. Not only with desire but something deeper. Something I refuse to even acknowledge, much less name.

I'll cling to this sweetness instead.

January wraps her arms around my neck, and the chair shifts as she lifts toward me. Her breasts are pressed into my chest, full and soft, and she's nipping at my mouth now, still mostly sugar with some chili pepper added.

I wrap my hands around her hips and pull her flush into me, her thighs hugging mine. The heat between us pulses, rises, and soon enough the sweetness is entirely burned away. She's panting into my mouth, her hands moving restlessly across my shoulders. My fingers tighten on her hips, so lush, and I bite her lower lip.

A stuttering moan leaves her throat. Jesus, but I love that sound.

When my phone rings, I hear it, but it doesn't quite penetrate my brain. There's only January and her body pressed against mine, her hands searching and needy, her mouth devouring mine.

When it rings again, I curse. I recognize that ring tone, and I have to answer it. *Motherfucker.*

I set January down on the desk, keeping one arm around her waist while I answer. If I can deal with this quickly, we can get back to what we were doing.

"Anjie." I try to sound happy to hear from her. "What's up?"

"Did I interrupt?"

Of course Anjie realizes she did. She reads people better than anyone I've ever met, and she knows all the Bastards like the back of her hand. Except for maybe Dev.

"No." I tighten my arm around January when she tries to wriggle away. "I wasn't up to anything. Much."

January runs her teeth along the side of my throat, making me gasp. It's half punishment, half sensual, and all turn-on.

"Really?" Anjie's skepticism is sharp in my ear. "Because it sounds like you're with someone."

Yes, the woman we're going to be giving millions of dollars to this morning. "What exactly do you need?" I put some steel into that. Not to chastise Anjie but more like I'm impatient to get back to work. When really I'm impatient to get back to January.

Anjie's probably already figured that out too.

"Ultra's lawyer has given the okay, but he hasn't heard back from January," she says. "Could you ask her if she's read his email yet?"

I go very, very still. "Like, right now?"

"If you could, please."

I close my eyes. It's like Anjie's got a line straight into our brains. I tuck my hand over the end of the phone. "Anjie wants to know if you've seen the lawyer's email," I whisper.

January's eyes go wide. *She knows?* she mouths.

I only nod. Anjie is a force of nature. It's like asking why a rainstorm keeps pouring.

"Um… yeah. Everything looks fine." January holds up her hands. *What do we do now?*

Apparently she doesn't want anyone to know about us. I haven't exactly been shouting it from the rooftops, but I don't care that Anjie knows. Anjie runs my life pretty much, as she does for the other Bastards. She's the one who arranged for the clothes yesterday. She's handled gifts and reservations for my dates before, but she's never teased me about them—which means she knows exactly how bad I have it for January.

There's a knock at the door. And there are the clothes for today.

"Can you get that?" I ask January. I smile, as charming as can be.

She stalks off to the door, still looking piqued.

I turn my attention back to the phone. "January says its fine." I drop my voice. "And Anjie, could you tone it down a little with her? She's…"

"Skittish?"

Skittish isn't right. More like wary. Afraid. I don't want her to have the slightest excuse to slip away from me.

"Maybe. Look, could you run a background check on her previous employers? All the funders, coworkers, and founders she's been around. See if you can find anyone who's suspicious."

Anjie's already done a background check on Ultra's current funders and employees. And followed up any whispers about potential buyers. Fuchs has supposedly been sniffing at them, but if he really had been, he would had offered January so much she'd have never come to us.

I suppose I ought to be grateful to the cold bastard.

"What's happened?" Anjie asks. "Is there something in particular I should be looking for?"

"No, just a hunch." More than a hunch—I know January's hiding something. She was hiding something this morning when I came in.

If she's going to hide things, I'm going to search them out. If I'm putting all this money and time into her company, I deserve to know everything. And maybe I can find out what's got her so spooked.

"All right," Anjie says. "I'll take care of it. Anything special I should order in for lunch today?"

"Hmm, maybe some of that roast chicken from the place in Bernal Heights? And something rich for dessert. Oh, and a bottle of Cristal."

There's a brief pause. Maybe I have surprised Anjie.

"Ooh, you do like her. How did she like the clothes?"

I hear January taking the clothes from the delivery man at that moment, pleased shock in her voice.

"She loves them," I say.

"You picked them out. I only did the ordering."

True, but I'm not telling January that. Let her think it's more magic.

I bid Anjie goodbye just as January walks back in, hugging the outfit to her chest. "Are you going to do this every day?" Even though she's rolling her eyes, there's a happy sparkle in her voice.

Suddenly I'm embarrassed like I haven't been since college. Because yeah, I do want to make her this happy every day.

"You'd run out of closet space," I say.

"Oh, I'm already out of that." She does a twirl, the skirt flaring out. "How did you know my size?"

"I have a practiced eye."

She goes very still, the skirt settling around her legs. "Of course."

"You're the only woman I've ever brought here." I say it because she looks sad—and like she's ready to bolt. I want her happy and by my side.

"Only? But this place is a seduction den."

"What the hell is a seduction den?"

"The picture windows, the breakfast ordered in, the stuff in the bathroom..." Her voice dies as realization dawns. "You really did all that for me."

I'm annoyed because she's seen too deep. I'm raw where's she looking. "I told you so." Instead of letting her dig deeper, I change the subject. "We're signing the papers today. Are you ready?"

She lets her arm fall, the skirt brushing the floor as she does. "I suppose I have to be."

I want something more from her—happiness, gratitude, undying devotion. Not what sounds like second thoughts.

I'll just have to work harder to impress her. To snare her as she's done to me. It's the only way to regain my balance with her.

CHAPTER 13

January

My second visit to Bastard Capital is somehow even more nerve-racking than the first.

It's not the money this time; it's Mark and how possessive he's being. Or maybe not possessive. He's not warning anyone off, but he is smiling at me, just for me, and occasionally touching me, like to remind himself he can.

Boyfriend-like, my stupid inner voice says. I tell her to be quiet because we haven't discussed anything like that.

He takes me through the building to his office, nodding to all the junior people along the way. He keeps his hand at the small of my back, a clear stamp of... something. And holy wow are there a ton of people working here.

Once we're in his office, he sits me on the sofa. A fresh cup of espresso in the most beautiful demitasse cup is already waiting for me.

"Can you sit tight while I make some calls?" he asks.

I only nod and fold my hands in my lap. Then I think better of it and pull out my laptop. I'm not going to sit here like the bored girlfriend dropping into the office against her will. I've got stuff to do too.

I pull up the Ultra Slack channel and enter the general chat room.

I'm here, getting ready to sign the papers!

Instantly Doc pings me back. *What is the office like? Is it as gorgeous as Mark?*

I glance at him from the corner of my eye. His expression is intense, stony as he talks into his phone. Whatever is going on, it's not a friendly call.

Somehow the heavy set of his brows and the firm line of his mouth turn me on. Of course. But he looks every inch a man not to fuck with, and what I can say? It's potent as all hell.

They have amazing coffee here, I type back. Doc doesn't need to know how gorgeous Mark is.

I heard they have one of those crazy Japanese drip systems and a full-time staffer just to run it.

Oh boy. *I haven't seen anything like that.* Not that it would surprise me if they did.

Did he get you new clothes today too?

Awesome. So Doc knows I spent another night with him.

I look down at the dress I'm wearing. It's a gorgeous slate blue that makes my skin glow and hugs my curves like it was custom made for me.

Maybe it was. Maybe Mark took my measurements when I was sleeping.

Yes. I don't elaborate. *What's up with the stack today?*

Hallie pops in then, followed by Meryem, and the chat is completely engulfed by work.

I sneak another glance at Mark and jump when I see he's watching me. There's so much heat in his gaze it's going to burn up all the oxygen in this room. Judging by how tight my lungs are, maybe it already has.

"You look incredible," he whispers to me.

I point to the phone in his hand. His smile twists into wickedness.

"Do you think they can hear me?" he asks.

I'm almost certain they can or at least know he's talking to someone else, whispering sweet nothings to her. But I also think he wants them to hear.

A frisson works its way down my spine. I want them to hear too. It's a little dangerous, and I have no idea who he's talking to, but I want them to know Mark Taylor is telling *me* I look incredible.

"I'm trying to work." I make that prim but also teasing.

"So am I."

Liar. Okay, maybe he is doing some work, but he's also trying to seduce me. In his office of all places.

But our first sex was on a desk. Maybe he wants to christen this desk too. We'd have to close all the curtains—two entire walls of his office are glass, one with a view of the corridors and one with a view of the atrium. I can see a man with a heavy beard, working in one of the offices across the atrium. I can't quite tell, but I think it's Finn. Elliot's got a beard too but not the wild tangle that Finn does. Finn looks like a lumberjack stuffed into a suit.

He catches me watching, and his teeth flash white in the middle of his beard. He even waves.

I can't do anything but wave back since he seems genuinely happy to see me.

"I'm going to have to tell Finn to stop flirting with you." Mark's voice is mild as water, but there's a bite of vinegar there too. Not that he'd ever choose me over his brothers.

"He's harmless." Compared to Mark, he's a damn teddy bear.

Mark snorts. "That's what he wants you to think."

"Are you scared?"

He sets the phone down, glancing up at me. "Of him? No."

Meaning that he's scared of me? But that's ridiculous. I'm about to sell him part of my company. Part of myself.

And I'm giving him all kinds of other parts of me when we're alone. He's got all the power here.

There's a short knock at the door. "Are you ready? Oh, she's already here!" The office manager greets me with a wide smile. I was expecting someone older, but she actually looks a few years younger than me. "We're so happy you're joining our family of start-ups!"

So this is the famous Anjie who knows I'm sleeping with Mark without him telling her.

Her hair is done in some kind of elaborate style from the thirties, her makeup is utterly flawless with ruler-straight eyeliner and the most perfect shade of red on her lips, and her silk dress has tiny angels and devils printed on it.

She's also got more tattoos than a sailor, winding down her arms and up her shoulders and chest. I wasn't quite sure what I was expecting in an office manager, but she wasn't it.

Mark smiles at her with deep friendliness and familiarity. Jealousy pulses through me. This woman is utterly gorgeous and works with him every day and gets smiles like that from him.

"Anjie," he says. "I know you've already got everything ready."

She winks at him. "Yep." She holds out a hand to me. Even her manicure is completely perfect. "I'm Anjelica, but you can call me Anjie. You must be January."

I shake with her, horribly aware of my one chipped nail. I would have fixed it, but Mark didn't think to include manicure supplies in his guest bathroom. "Um, yes. Thanks for arranging this and getting me the meeting..."

And the clothes and I guess you know that I'm sleeping with him, which I don't know how to feel about.

Anjie tucks my hand into her elbow as if we're old

friends. "Don't mention it. I'm glad we'll have some more women around here. And I love your dress."

A nasty thought occurs to me. "You picked it out, didn't you?"

"Pfft. Mark did. I only ordered it."

Mark groans. "Thank you, Anjie. That'll be all."

She winks at me now. "He's so cute when he's flustered. But you already knew that. And I'm so glad you two were able to reconnect."

We both go still.

"Reconnect?" I ask.

Anjie lets me go, propping a hand against her hip. "Well, yeah, you knew each other in college. Mark's talked about you of course."

Mark talked about me. Before I asked for a meeting. Anjie knew about college.

I don't even know how to process that. Judging by the expression on Mark's face, he doesn't either.

Anjie isn't finished. "So when you called for a meeting, I made sure Mark would be there."

I should be angry or maybe shocked, but she looks so pleased I feel instead as if I've been hit with a fairy godmother's wand. Not one of the nice fairy godmothers but one of the more modern, snarky ones.

"Thanks, Anjie," Mark says dryly. "I'm glad you always know what's best for me."

"Of course." Her smile never dims. "I'll just get everyone else, and we can start signing."

Once she's gone, I send Mark a look. "So, we've been managed, hmm?"

He sends me one much more intense, hotter than the one I'm giving him. "Are you complaining?"

No. No, I don't think I am. I suppose I'll have to get used to being managed by Anjie too once I sign those papers.

Like a good little minion, I head out to the conference room.

The Bastards assembled together in one room is quite a sight. A really hot sight, although Mark is hottest of all. There's Logan, desperately beautiful but also with an air of sadness. I remember Callie and how strained she'd looked, like she was about to shatter. Logan has the same look in his eyes.

Then comes Finn, who couldn't be more different from Logan. He's got a massive beard, eyes that never stop twinkling, and a nose that's been broken more than a few times. The press is always referring to him as the redneck programmer, which makes him sound like a rube. But he's not—he might be the smartest guy in this room, at least in terms of pure coding genius. Rumor has it he used to hack into the NSA in college, just to leave memes on their computers.

Paul is sitting next to Finn, looking suave as all get out. He's the money man, the one who provided the stake for the first test of their stock market algorithm, the test that made them all rich. He's also the most pedigreed one here, coming from a family with long-standing wealth. But he's taken his inheritance and increased it a hundredfold. He's no lazy trust fund baby.

Elliot is across the table from them, sitting on his own. He's the one who doesn't belong even though he's Logan's brother. As far as I know, he's never typed a line of code in his life; he's a lawyer. *Their* lawyer, to be specific. He's wearing heavy glasses and a three-piece suit in gray tweed, but he's not going for a hipster vibe at all. No, he's wearing that entire getup completely unironically, as if looking like an extra straight out of some Jimmy Stewart film is exactly how a lawyer of today should be. It would be adorable if not for the expression on his face, which is pinched and scowling. Like he's very upset at this interruption in his routine.

The way he's set up his pens and paper, everything exactly parallel, proves it.

And finally there is Dev. The mysterious one. He's in jeans and a T-shirt, same as Mark and Finn, but somehow on him they look more like monk's robes. Maybe because of the intense depth of his gaze. There are secrets in Dev's eyes, secrets he's not going to let anyone see.

I wonder how many of those secrets the other Bastards know. I'll never find out since Mark would never tell even if I asked. These men are brothers with a bond deeper than blood. I can sense it humming between them, tying them together.

Dev is watching me, and I want to squirm even though they're all glancing at me. But something about his gaze is unsettling and not in a good way, although he looks relaxed. It makes me want to grab Mark's hand to remind Dev that I'm not the enemy.

Anjie sets a coffee in front of him, and he suddenly crackles like a live wire, tension snapping off him. He's not paying any attention to me anymore.

"Here you go," she chirps, only there's an edge to it she didn't have with anyone else. I can't tell if they hate each other or are desperately in lust.

Interesting.

Anjie brings me a cup, and I do a double take. Any other company would have given out a heavy mug with their logo stamped on it, but this cup is of the thinnest china, the rim edged with gold and stylized blue hibiscus running down the bowl. There's even a saucer, which is just as pretty as the cup.

I take a sip and… *Dear Lord.*

People often joke about the ten-dollar cups of coffee in San Francisco, but this coffee is worth ten dollars and then some. It's the first cup I've ever had where I can taste the care that went into roasting the beans and brewing the coffee. I'd be tempted to sell my firstborn for this coffee.

The rest of them are sipping from their cups as if it's no big deal, as if they get coffee that wonderful every day. And they probably do.

Finn's cup looks ridiculous in his huge, battered hands, too dainty against his lumberjack beard. But Mark...

I force myself not to sigh with delight. Mark drinks his with a rough grace that makes my bones melt. The cup is small in his hands, but not silly, and he holds it as if the beauty of it is his due. Nothing to boast or brag about, but simply *his*.

Elliot sits up, although I never would have guessed his earlier posture was his version of slouching. He clears his throat and adjusts his papers. "Thank you," he murmurs to Anjie when she sets a coffee cup in front of him. "Should we begin?"

Everyone assumes a stony expression, even Mark. It's business time then. I can see what he means about not letting our... *relationship* interfere with this deal. These men all mean the utmost seriousness.

I arrange myself better, not letting my nerves show. This is even more important to me than it is to them. "Yes. I'm ready."

Elliot passes a thick stack of legal papers to me, the lines and lines of lawyer speak looking like marching ants. "As you can see, we'll be assuming a thirty percent stake in Ultra shares for five million dollars."

Five million is small change for every man at this table, but my heart jumps at the number. That amount will keep Ultra going for a while.

I have the time and money now to stop Fuchs. My throat starts to close as emotion overwhelms me, but I clench my teeth and force myself to keep breathing. Now's not the time.

Everyone's waiting for me to respond, to do something beyond try not to cry. "Yes." I inwardly roll my eyes. *Great response, January.* "That's great news for Ultra. And for you since our encryption system will be second to none."

Mark catches my eye and smiles with one side of his mouth, small but devastating. That really makes me want to cry since the urge to tell him everything is burning in my chest. I have the money, but I still want him on my side. By my side.

"That's what we're counting on," he says. The light in his eyes says he truly believes it. "And in light of our relationship, Dev will handle matters relating to any sale of Ultra stock on our end or the decision to make an initial public offering."

Our relationship?

Everyone stares steadily back at me. I swallow hard as I realize they all know we're sleeping together. I guess they inferred a lot from those pictures of us at Alcatraz in *TidBytes*. And whatever Mark might have told them.

Relationship. I mean, I used that word before, in the privacy of my own mind, but that, um, sounds more permanent than sleeping together.

Is this his way of saying that we're *together*-together?

I knew from the very beginning I was way in over my head with this man, but now the waves are crashing, threatening to drown me. I'm not ready to swim for the shore yet though. Because I want to be *together*-together too.

I think. If only I could trust Mark with all my secrets—

"Ms. Harris?" Elliot prompts. "Is that agreeable to you?"

They're all staring back at me as if it's totally normal for Mark to be doing a business deal with his lover. Except Finn has a grin that clearly says *Yeah, get some!*

I bite my lip and drop my head to keep from laughing.

"Yeah, that makes sense." I clear my throat. "No, it's exactly right."

I look at Dev, who's as blank-faced as if we were talking about turnip varieties or something. But when Mark catches my eye, I can tell he's trying not to laugh too. He sends me a wink that warms me from the inside out.

"So where do I sign?" I ask Elliot.

CHAPTER 14

She's all mine now.

Rather, her company is, but with the way she's looking at me as we step into my living room makes me believe that she is too. It's like I planned this room specifically to be a frame for her. Like I was waiting for her all this time.

Maybe I was.

The papers are all signed, the champagne's been drunk, and we're coming back from an intimate dinner at a hole-in-the-wall Italian place a block from my house. It's not my private club, but I can tell she's charmed by my friendly relationship with the owners.

January's charmed by everything today, her attitude since the signing one of happy brightness. I can't see any secrets in her eyes.

So where have they gone? Or was it only concern about her funding, and now that she has it, she has me right where she wants me?

I put those thoughts away and force my mood to lighten up. So what if she was more concerned with the funding— she's here tonight.

"Should I open another bottle of champagne?" I ask as I toss my jacket across the sofa.

January opens her arms to the view of the bay, looking as if she's about to take flight. "I've had more than enough. I have to work tomorrow and start earning back your investment."

I don't bother to tell her that five million is nothing to us. "Not until tomorrow though. I have other plans for you tonight."

She giggles, and the sound rolls through me all the way to my heels. I can't remember the last time someone actually *giggled* at me.

"Should we be contacting Dev?" she asks. Her saucy grin makes my cock stir. "So that he knows we're committing coitus?"

One corner of my mouth curls up. "No. Dev is the last person I want to involve. And *committing coitus?*"

If there was ever a way to kill a man's erection stone dead, it'd be those words. But my desire for her is more powerful than that, an all-consuming thing that demands I have her now.

She shifts and stretches, clearly feeling the champagne. She's gone lanky, languid, and oh so sexy.

"Now that it's all official," she says, "it feels so much more illicit. Doesn't it?"

It actually doesn't. It feels more real, more solid, now that our relationship is in the open. The papers are all signed, the Bastards all know—this is the most real relationship I've had in years.

I won't let that realization shake me.

"You wish no one knew about it?" I raise an eyebrow. "Not very ethical, Miss Harris."

"Sometimes secrets can be fun. Sexy." A cloud passes over

her face, as if the secrets she's thinking of aren't those things at all.

Damn. And here I thought that was behind her. In a way, I was hoping she was only worried about the money, because that was one thing I could definitely give her.

Whatever else she's hiding, the reasons she has for being so desperate for help, I can't know. Anjie's sleuthing never found anything, and my power in this world only goes so far. I get almost everything I want but can't read her mind no matter how badly I want to.

I want her to be happy, carefree again, so I distract her. "What sexy secrets do you have?"

She shakes her head. "None. I'm sadly boring."

That's a damn lie. She's the most fascinating woman I've ever met. And she's most definitely got secrets.

Anjie got her report back to me today. There's nothing new there—everything's on the up-and-up with her previous companies, and the rumors about Fuchs offering for Ultra aren't anything more than whispers. Although Fuchs has been buying up lots of encryption companies lately—probably to sell the tech to the CIA and NSA. He'd be an ideal buyer for Ultra if he was interested.

January's committed to selling her tech to some phone company and using it to protect ordinary people, but I'm not convinced they actually need it. The world's most powerful encryption on pictures of your kids? It just doesn't make sense. Once she sees the size of her cut, realizes the life it will give her, she'll say yes. They always do. Idealists don't last long here. Not the real ones.

I want January to last though. I don't want this place to chew her up and spit her out like it does to so many others. Hell, I want to be her own personal shield.

Finally I stop lying to myself. I'm falling for her all over again. And I'm terrified all over again.

Logan let someone in, thought they'd be in love forever, and then she broke him. I know January is here for funding, know that she's got secrets, ones I can't unearth even with all my contacts—I'd be a fool to fall in love with her.

No. No, I'd be a fool to let her *know* I'm falling for her, that she has that power over me. We can continue on as we are—blazing hot sex, me showering her with gifts—but until she comes clean, until we sell her company and the money issue isn't between us, I'm not going to be vulnerable. I learned my lesson in college with her.

"What's wrong?" Her eyes are tight with worry.

I smooth out my expression. "Nothing. The usual work bullshit."

"Oh. What's—" She shakes her head, catches herself. "Of course you can't tell me. Your NDA is ironclad."

True. But there can't be much of a line between work and our relationship, not with how obsessed we both are with our careers. I'm going to be there tomorrow in her office, working right alongside her, and will be until her encryption system sells.

"It's nothing for you to worry about. I don't want you to worry about a thing when you're with me."

The shadows under her eyes lighten, something like hope chasing them away. "I—"

Her breath catches, and the moment suspends between us.

She's finally going to tell me.

My heart catches too, reaching out to her. *Trust me. Tell me.*

"I don't worry when I'm with you."

Maybe she's lying, but I want to believe her, so I do.

"Good." I seize her hand and pull her into me. Her curves are soft and her skin is silk, and she smells like my dream of a woman. "God, but you're so fucking gorgeous."

She wraps her arms around my neck and presses her lips to mine, her tongue tracing the seam of my lips. Her desire is as hot and urgent as mine, which only fuels the fire in me. No matter how hot we burn together, it feels like it will never be enough.

"I need you," she says against my lips, into my throat, along my collarbone. I've never had a woman so hungry for me.

"Come to bed with me."

She pulls away, her breath catching and her eyes wide. "Your bed?"

I nod, then pull her in for another kiss. I can't tell her that I've been dreaming about her in my bed. I don't want her searching gaze on me, burrowing into mine. She sees too much, and I don't want her seeing too much into this.

Although it is a pretty big deal, inviting her to my bed. But I won't let slip how big of a deal it is. That way it won't mean anything to her, and my secrets will remain safe.

I want her in my bed, and I get what I want. It's that simple.

I take her hand, lead her down the hall and up the stairs. "I haven't given you the grand tour, have I?"

Really, besides the living room, office, and my bedroom, there's not much else to the house. Some guest bedrooms, a gym, and a rooftop deck with a view as amazing as the one in the living room.

I'll have to arrange a private dinner for us on that deck one of these nights. Or maybe some morning. Yes, that's what I'll do, have a chef come in and make a mind-blowing brunch for us. Dinner's too predictable. Brunch will surprise her.

"No," she says. "Is that what we're doing now?"

I push open my bedroom door and shake my head. "Not tonight. I have other plans."

The shimmer that goes through her makes my cock hard as steel. So beautiful, so sexy, so responsive. And so damn smart. If I were looking for the perfect woman, she might be it.

If.

Her hand goes to the zipper of her dress. "Plans? That sounds interesting."

There's the slightest of snicks, a few teeth of the zipper releasing. But she holds it to only a few, teasing me.

I take a spot in the armchair in the corner, flicking on the table lamp as I do. The light is soft, caressing, a perfect frame for her.

"Interesting is one way to put it." I gesture to her dress. "I think you forgot to finish something."

Her chin lifts. She's thinking about defying me.

Oh, sweet January, if that's the game you want to play...

Then her chin drops, all coy submission, and the back of her dress opens like a flower. She shimmies out of it.

I take a short, sharp breath, embarrassingly close to a gasp. But damn it, I can't help it, because she's a fucking vision. The black lace cups of her bra hold her breasts high and tight, and I can glimpse the dark curls between her legs behind the lace of her panties.

I run a hand down my cock, spread my legs. Fuck, that feels good.

"So this is where the magic happens." January is looking around the room, her gaze coming back to the bed again and again.

It's an impressive bed. The frame is solid oak, waxed to a high sheen, and the mattress is raised high enough to be a throne. The sheets are like sleeping on an angel's robe.

She can't look away, her tongue coming out to wet her lips. She's imagining so many things on that bed, her and me and sweat and needs, I can tell.

Lucky for her, I can make all those fantasies real. Lucky for me too.

"Get on the bed," I say.

She raises an eyebrow but does it, her long limbs making me picture them wrapped around me. Soon enough, we'll get to that. January perches on the edge, then leans back, her breasts high and her legs a straight line to her pussy.

"You're going to stay all the way over there?" she asks.

"Mmm." I shift my legs, making more room for my growing erection. "Touch yourself."

She lifts one hand, sets it lightly on her collarbone. I can see her pulse thrumming at the base of her throat.

"Is that where you want to be touched?" I ask, my voice rough.

"I want to be touched all over."

"Show me."

She runs both hands over her torso, down her arms, and then cups her breasts, squeezing hard and biting her lip. Her nipples jut out through the fabric.

I palm my cock as I take her in. She's a work of art, an erotic muse made flesh. I want to grab her and never let go. But her touching herself is too damn hot to stop now.

When her fingers find her nipples and pull, I groan like I'm dying. "Jesus."

One corner of her mouth tips up. She knows what she does to me.

"Again," I say.

She does, and it's even more potent this time, her fingers sure and certain as she teases herself. I'm sure and certain I could come just from watching her. Already my cock is pulling toward the waistband of my pants, demanding to be released. I can feel the wetness at the tip.

"You like that." It's not a question or a tease from her. More like she's as lost in this as I am.

I stroke myself. "I do. And so do you."

She releases her nipples and lets her hand trail down her belly, the skin there as soft as my sheets. "I really want to be touched here though."

When her legs spread and her fingers rub over the crotch of her panties, I can see the dampness spreading through the fabric and along her thighs. Her skin gleams with it.

The urge to go to her, to bury my face between her legs, is almost unstoppable. But I hold back. I want her out of her mind, and losing my own control isn't the way to do that.

"How wet are you?" I ask. I can see for myself, but I want to hear her say it.

"Soaked." Her fingers dip under the edge of her panties. "And my clit is swollen. It almost hurts to touch."

But she continues to stroke it, and I can just *see* how slick and throbbing it must be. As slick as my cock is, still trapped in my pants.

"Take the panties off. Take all of it off." It feels like I'm speaking through gravel, my voice as low and rough as the things I want to do to her.

January doesn't bother to be coy as she unhooks her bra and kicks off her panties. My heart races into overdrive. I squeeze my cock through my pants, trying to take the edge off. But there's no relief there, not when January is sitting back on the bed again, her feet on the floor, her knees open just enough for me to glimpse her sweet pink folds.

"You want to watch?" she asks. She runs a languid hand across her pussy lips, more teasing than anything.

"For now."

"Mmm." She makes a small growl of pleasure, her breasts bobbing as she reaches between her legs, her hand more insistent now.

I watch as she slips one finger inside, slowly working at

herself, her thumb finding her clit. Another growl of pleasure from her, her hand working faster.

This is so fucking hot that my brain is about to explode into flames and send fire sizzling down every one of my nerve endings.

She slips another finger in, her hand speeding up, groans falling from her lips even as she bites down to keep them inside.

My own hand is working nearly as fast even though my cock is still trapped behind too many layers of fabric. *Don't fucking do it,* I warn my oncoming climax. *Watch her.*

My iron control is rewarded when she comes with a scream that rattles the windows, her skin pink and damp all over, just like the deep, delicate folds of her pussy. Her breasts quiver deliciously with every shuddering breath, and I'm transported by the sight.

Jesus God, just remembering this could keep me hot in a blizzard.

But when she opens her eyes, the entire scene shifts. No longer is she a slave to her pleasure. No, now she's fully in control.

Her next words cement that notion: "I want to see you."

CHAPTER 15

He might have bought a huge stake in my company today, but he's the one who's given up more than he knows.

I'm in his room, and while I might be the naked one, he's exposed himself by bringing me here. And I'm going to crack him open even further until I'm as deeply burrowed within his thoughts as he is in mine.

My skin is flushed and glowing with my orgasm; the aftershocks still pulsing through me make me feel powerful.

"I want to see you," I demand.

For the first time, I catch him off guard. His eyes flicker as his chest tenses, throwing his amazing pecs into even sharper relief.

He reaches for the hem of his shirt with eagerness. I feel like we've crossed some kind of bridge here in his bedroom with him getting naked for me without even a hint of hesitation. It wasn't that he was hiding something or that he didn't want me to see him naked—it was only that it had to really matter.

I gasp, partly at his amazing chest and arms, which are now exposed, and partly at my own realization. This isn't simply sex between us, not that it ever really was. Each step that we take from now on will lead us deeper into what we're becoming together.

I stalk closer to him, holding out my hand to touch. His skin is hot, almost feverish, the muscle beneath as tense as the cables holding up the Golden Gate Bridge. There's some hair, just enough to be delightfully prickly.

"Your body is amazing."

He's holding his breath, perhaps to hold himself back from kissing me, but he pulls in a rasping lungful to answer. "The gym helps me think."

"Mmm." I press my fingers hard into the wall of muscle, letting my nails scratch slightly. "You must spend a lot of time thinking."

He doesn't even smile. His jaw is way too tight for that. All that desire, all that power, and he's only barely holding it back.

I run my index finger down his chest, along his abs, and follow the trail of hair that disappears into his waistband. He's breathing again, hard, serrated pants that reveal how thin his control really is.

I tap the buckle of his belt with my nail, *snick snick snick.* He jumps with every touch.

"All of it, please," I say.

I lean back to give him room. He can't take his eyes off me as he jerks off his pants and then his boxer briefs, his gaze like green fire. It makes me think of dragons and knights and maidens being ravished.

He's no knight and I'm no maiden, but he's definitely about to ravish me.

When he sprawls back in the chair in all his naked glory, my knees go weak. His abs are chiseled like a Greek statue's, his thighs are like tree trunks, and his cock...

I swallow hard. I've had his cock deep within me, yet seeing it for the first time is still a shock. He's got the cock of a sex god, thick and long, the veins stark as they run up his shaft to the swollen purple head. His balls are heavy and weighty beneath their nest of hair.

The sight isn't beautiful, not at all. It's powerful and primal and raw, the same as how he fucks.

I drop to one knee, then the other, bracing myself on his thighs. His cock bobs and hardens right before my eyes. Wetness collects in my pussy, slicks my thighs. I press my knees hard together, my clit jumping as I do.

Mark's hands find the arms of the chair and dig in deep. My own fingers dig into his thighs, bracing us both as I lean forward and take his cock in my mouth.

Blow jobs have never been a favorite of mine. I feel stupid on my knees, my mouth full, and sometimes the taste... isn't to my taste.

Giving Mark a blow job is another thing entirely. My mouth is full of *him*, he tastes like pure sex, and the grunts he's making land right in my clit, *bam bam bam.* I tighten my thighs and increase the pressure. Lord, it's like he's fingering me without even touching me.

He doesn't grab my head or my neck—which is something I hate. Mark, the man who can have the entire tech world tremble with a frown, simply grips the chair and lets me set the pace and depth. The muscles in his thighs shake under my hands, his cock swelling and jerking as I take him deep, then draw back, then take him deep again.

My clit is aching now, my thighs stretched to the breaking point as I squeeze and squeeze and squeeze. A low thrum takes hold of my clit, deep pulses of pleasure spreading throughout me.

Holy crap, I'm going to have an orgasm *while giving him a blow job.*

I come up for a quick breath of air, to grab my bearings, but Mark is too fast. He pulls me into his lap, my thighs straddling his. His fingers find my pussy, push deep, even as his teeth find my nipple.

My scream is even louder this time because this orgasm comes on so fast, so hard, it almost hurts. But it's the best kind of pain.

The afterglow has barely started when he takes my knee and drapes it over the arm of the chair, doing the same with the other. The arms are low enough that it's still comfortable, but I'm completely exposed, unable to easily move my hips.

He's going to have to take the lead here, which I'm sure was his intention all along.

Mark wraps a hand around my nape, holding me steady. He's found a condom somewhere and already put it on. His other hand is at my hip, his cock pushing forward, filling me, the position making the sensation almost too much to bear.

He says nothing as he moves, surging into me, then retreating, then returning to fill me again. He only holds my nape and my gaze, the intensity there threatening to burn me.

But I *am* burning, all of me surrendering to the heat between us as he pumps into me, grunting his pleasure with every thrust. Our skin slaps together, his thighs against mine, his balls against my ass. It's all so raw, so primal, but so intimate at the same time.

When he comes, his body shuddering with his release, I come too. This last orgasm is as intense as the others and leaves me completely wrung out.

I fold over him, grateful for his strong arms that grab me. I don't have to worry about staying upright when he's here to catch me.

"My sweet January," he whispers in my ear.

I'm too far gone after my third orgasm to answer him. Instead, I press my face deeper into his neck, tasting the salt on his skin and smelling the musk clinging to both of us.

Mark gathers me close and carries me to the bed. "Get some sleep," he says as he tucks me in.

Some sputter through my brain makes me open my mouth. He needs to stay with me, only I can't make my mouth work. I'm already drifting into dreams.

But then his arm comes around me, my back meeting his chest as he tucks me under his chin.

Finally things are perfect.

So I sleep.

CHAPTER 16

Work is amazing today. The weather is amazing today. Everything is just fucking amazing.

When Finn comes into my office, I smile at him, thinking he's here to shoot the shit. Sounds good to me too.

And then he's followed by Paul, Elliot, and Dev—but not Logan—and my mood turns in an instant, because I already know what they're here for.

"I thought we agreed January and I being together wouldn't be a problem," I say flatly.

Finn spins around a chair and straddles it. "You sleeping with her isn't a problem. You falling in love with her..." He waggles a finger. "Now that's a problem."

Love. That's not what I feel for January. It can't be. Except my heart keeps doing weird things while the word *love* keeps echoing through my brain.

"She's not like Callie." That's way too defensive, but it's true. And that's really what they're worried about—that I'll end up like Logan, married and miserable.

"No, we know that," Finn says. They all nod along. "Shit, Callie wouldn't even walk into the offices, much less talk shop with us. She made it clear Logan was hers, not ours.

But... but if she leaves you, we can't have two zombies walking around here."

Logan's not a zombie, but he is pretty fucked up, thanks to his wife. "I'm not in love with January."

"You had a thing for her in college," Paul says softly.

"None of us are who we were in college," I say. "We've all been through too much since. Together."

"We don't think you'll end up like Logan," Dev says. "But... we want to consul caution here—"

"We don't want you to get hurt," Finn cuts in bluntly.

My heart does some more weird things, because I really do love these guys. I'd never say so openly, because that's mushy bullshit, which we don't do, but the emotion is there. I'd kill for them, and they'd do the same for me.

"January and I both know the score here." *Love*, my idiot subconscious says. Stupid fucking hindbrain. "I've got it under control. I've seen Logan too."

Elliot clears his throat. "All that being said, she seems incredibly sharp."

A look passes between all of them.

"Hell, you fuckers actually *like* her," I say, realization dawning.

"Well, yeah, we like her," Paul says. "But we like you better."

"Aww, that's so sweet. I feel so loved."

Finn rolls his eyes as he gets up. "Forget it. I told you this asshole wouldn't appreciate our efforts."

"No, come on guys, group hug," I call as they head for the door. "Hey, wait."

The seriousness of my tone has them stopping.

"Something's got January spooked. I can't tell what, but... there's something there."

Dev's gaze is darkly intense. "Background research didn't bring anything up?"

I shake my head. "Nothing. But if you could keep an ear out for anything, I'd appreciate it. I don't want her..."

I stop before I reveal too much about how I care for January.

These guys have always known me too well though.

"Don't want her to be scared? Or upset?" Paul asks. Understanding softens his expression.

"Yeah," is all I say.

They don't say anything more—no more teasing or insults—they all just nod as one. My brothers, agreeing to help protect my lady.

Once they're gone, I grab my coat and head up to the City, eager to see January. Because I can't stop thinking about how hot she is, not because I'm in love with her or any shit like that.

When I arrive in SoMa, Roasted Café is hopping at lunchtime, like usual.

This is the place to see and be seen in the tech world—I count at least ten CEOs sitting in here, a couple of VCs, and of course dozens of start-up founders, all looking to catch the eye of a CEO or VC. I'm only here to grab some coffee and a bagel for January before I head over to the Ultra offices, not looking to meet new talent.

In a corner table, I spy Arne Fuchs nursing a cup of coffee along with some of his employees. Arne, who's very invested in his routines, has lunch here every day at twelve thirty. The staff know to keep that table clear for him.

The employees he's invited along are there to defend their projects from his keen eye. This won't be a restful lunch for them, not with Arne picking apart every last detail they give him.

If he's eating alone, it means none of his staff have impressed him enough to get an invite. I wonder what his employees would say was worse: getting invited or being left out. I haven't done a deal with him before, because he's a weird fucker and supposedly a high-functioning sociopath—I don't want to deal with his issues.

But if the price were right for Ultra, I could handle whatever weird shit he's into, as long as it came with a cool billion or two.

I grab January's coffee from the counter and head out. But on my way to the door, Fuchs waves me over to his table.

For a moment I'm tempted to wave back and keep going. Fuck him if he thinks he can summon me like one of his minions. But then I get my temper under control. I need to be good cop here in case he's got something interesting for me.

Or if I might have something interesting for him.

The knot of employees around him scatters as I approach. He must have told them to get lost. They look relieved to be leaving.

"Hey, Arne." I don't sit down because I don't want January's coffee to get cold.

Fuchs stares up at me like he's been trained to make eye contact rather than it coming naturally. As far as tech dudes go, he's one of the weirder ones. There's rumors that he's obsessed with living forever and he tries every life-extension trick out there: caloric restriction, sleeping in a special pressure chamber, and even getting a blood transfusion from a younger source every few days.

If that's what it takes to live forever, I'll take a shorter, happier life span any day.

Weirdness isn't a deal breaker here in the valley though. Arne has been behind several billion-dollar launches, and Corvus is currently rumored to be worth several billion—he can obsess over living forever all he wants and still be welcomed in our circles, as long he keeps making that kind of money.

"Mark," he says slowly. "I enjoyed the party."

I don't think he did, but manners are manners. "Great. What did you need?" There's no need for chitchat, not when we're only acquaintances at best. I lift the coffee cup. "I'm kind of in a rush."

His expression flickers, possibly because we're all in a rush. Or maybe because he thinks I ought to be more grateful for his attention. Fuchs is not a conversationalist—if he takes time to speak with you, it's supposedly a big deal.

Well, I'm a big deal around here too. I keep my smile fixed and a touch vague, the better to hurry him along.

"Where are you off to?"

I can't tell if Fuchs is generally curious or if he's only practicing his human interaction. "We've recently invested in Ultra. I'm off to mind the shop."

There's nothing in his expression, not even a flicker. "Yes, I did see. Congratulations. Or rather, congratulations to the company. You have a knack for choosing winners."

I incline my head, because I'm not going to be falsely modest—I really do. "January Harris, the founder—she's onto something big."

Here's the point where Fuchs should show his hand, because this is the real reason he's called me over. Corvus has been picking up encryption companies lately, and it looks like maybe he's got an interest in Ultra. It's way too soon to be thinking about an offer, but that doesn't matter. The game only requires a mild show of interest here.

Except Fuchs doesn't know how to play the game. He does nothing at all except go back to his coffee. "I won't keep you waiting then."

I don't roll my eyes, although the urge is strong. It's not his fault he's better at coding and terrifying his employees than speaking the secret language of deals in Silicon Valley. He's a weirdo, sure, especially with the life-extension stuff, but otherwise mostly harmless. His money is as good as the next CEO's and maybe even better when it comes to Ultra.

"See you," I say, then head for the door.

But mentally I stick Corvus in my potential buyer file for Ultra. We've got a lot of work still to do before that, but that's not going to stop me from thinking several moves ahead.

CHAPTER 17

January

Mark isn't here, which makes me sad.

And that makes me irritated. It's my office, my company —of course he isn't here. Which is good, because I have tons of work to do. Except I'm not doing it.

Instead, I'm browsing through the Bletchley Circle group, trying to solve a few of the easier codes. I've been so busy with Ultra that I'm out of practice. Turns out that working on encryption in real life isn't so helpful with encryption games.

I'm distracted too since my brain keeps forcing me to look at the front door, just in case Mark is on his way. I woke up in his bed this morning, with his arms around me, and now I'm staring at the door like a teenager.

Okay, so I might be falling for him. Which feels giddy and amazing, but it's also a terrible, stupid thing to do.

Yes, he's into me. *Very* into me. But once my encryption system sells, will that be it?

I don't want it to end then, but I have no idea how he might feel.

Doc pops her head into my cubicle. "Have you seen the new building they have for us?"

I summon a smile and try not to look at the door. The new office is another extravagance, an entire floor in a high-rise with stunning views of the bay, and Blue Bottle not half a block away, along with several high-end cafés favored by the tech elite. We're moving to a deluxe apartment in the sky, as the song goes.

"It's amazing."

"Um, yeah." Doc shakes her head. She can't understand why I'm not more excited. And I am; I'm just more excited by whatever's happening between Mark and me. "I've been going over the floor plan, and I've already got everything mapped out. Do you think we'll want a server farm?"

I raise my eyebrows. "There's room for a server farm?"

A server farm is usually a ginormous room filled with computers all connected to each other, the better to increase their computational power. The room is also climate controlled at a very frosty temperature—all that processing generates a lot of heat. It's not something you throw together.

Doc whips out her tablet. A floor plan is on the screen. "Boom. Server farm, right there."

Sure enough, there's a room labeled SERVER FARM on the floor. It isn't enough space for a huge one, but it's better than renting time on an off-site one like we've been.

"Sure," I say weakly. "Why not? We've got the money. Who's going to manage it though?"

"Don't worry, Meryem has already said it'd be her baby." Doc studies the floor plan, then looks up at me. Worry crosses her face. "Everything okay? You seem way too anxious about this."

I want to tell her that I'm *still* anxious, that while we have plenty of money, it still hasn't solved the central problem of Fuchs's evil plan and Grace. But it's safer for Doc if she doesn't know.

I shrug. "Usual founder's blues. We're entering the Valley of Despair."

The Valley of Despair is what we call the few months right after a big infusion of capital, as a company comes down from the high of getting a massive pile of cash and has to get down to the dirty work of making a functional product that consumers will actually use.

Doc blows a raspberry. "Dude, we're already so close. Hallie got the chip prototypes back from the lab, and they're blowing her away. Imogen's debugging code like a fiend, and I'd say we're ready for an alpha launch in a month. Maybe less."

An alpha version is the version you get before even a beta version. It's buggy, half-finished, and not meant for anyone outside the tech bubble. But it's still a great accomplishment.

But a month is pretty far away.

That's not Doc's concern though or anyone else's. They're already working to the utmost limit. "Great," I say. "You guys are miracle workers."

"So are you." Doc waggles her eyebrows. "Both with the funding and the significant other. It's all over *TidBytes*."

I groan. "Do I want to know?"

Doc grins. "It's actually pretty nice. Calls you the luckiest woman in tech for securing the Bastards' support and for snaring Mark Taylor. There's a nice picture of you two leaving some bar in the Marina." Doc can't help her instinctive shudder—her loathing for that neighborhood is stronger than her happiness for me.

"It was a nice bar."

"Lord, spare me from *nice* bars. But listen." She goes very serious. "Is this all… legit with Mark? Not that you're faking," she says quickly, "but is everything okay with you two and him funding the company and all that? I don't want you to get hurt."

I swallow hard. Doc instantly wraps me in her arms.

"It's okay," I say, sniffling. "I'm just touched is all."

"I'm serious. If you're only with him for the money, we don't need it that bad."

"We do, but that's not why I'm with him. He's…"

Doc stares at me as I try to find the words. It was lust and tension before, but it feels like more. And I don't know if it's safe to let it be more.

"He's great," I say finally, then I giggle, because it sounds so silly.

Doc lets me go as she shakes her head. "You're fucking gone, chica. Head over heels." She moves to the door. "I'm here if you need me though."

"Thanks. But I promise I'll be fine."

Doc gives me one last pat on the shoulder, and then she heads back to her workstation.

I try to get back to work since we're now only a month away from something big, but again I can't focus. My mind darts from my puzzles to Mark to Grace back to my encryption program and never settles on any one thing. I'm all scrambled.

And then my messaging app pings.

Not the one that everyone and their mother uses—the special one I coded just for Grace, the one I disguised as a dictionary.

Holy hell, Grace is trying to message me. I almost drop the phone I'm so eager to see what she's written.

The app seems to take forever to load, the welcome screen mocking me with its blankness. And then:

Hi.

I want to cry and scream and laugh all at once. Grace hasn't said a word to me for months, and she opens with hi?

Hey yourself, I send back. *How are you?*

I'm safe.

I close my eyes and send up a prayer of thanks. *Can you tell me where you are?*

No.

Okay. I knew that was probably what she'd say, but my breath still catches sharply.

Grace sends me another message without waiting for my reply. *He's buying every encryption company he can. He sends the employees here, to the Spiderweb.*

The Spiderweb is the code name for his spyware division.

To do what? I ask. I don't know if she can answer that either though.

So he can break any encryption in use.

He's already planned for my attack, and he's preemptively killing any company that can pose a threat.

Well, he's not getting us. I'm going to fight until the end. Thank God he only made us a private offer, one I could refuse in private. I'll just have to keep denying him without the Bastards finding out. Fuchs's legendary secretiveness will help me out too; he's not going to go mouthing off about how I turned him down or even that he offered for Ultra.

Thank you, I send to Grace. *Now I know what to expect. Are we on his radar?*

We?

Oh God, she doesn't even know about Ultra. He must be censoring their internet access.

I have a company. An encryption company. I started it because of...

I don't know how to finish that. So far, our conversation is fairly innocent or at least could be spun that way. Admitting that she sent me private documents, even over a secure line, would be stupid.

Because of you, I finish.

There's a long pause. Too long.

You can't do that.

Although you can't read tone into a text message, I can sense her frustration, her fear.

Don't cross him—you can't fight him. No one can. Stay quiet, keep the evidence hidden.

There's nothing more after that. I watch my phone for the rest of the day, hours and hours spent just staring.

There's nothing more.

Then, finally, Mark shows up, a smile on his face and plans for dinner for us, and I'm forced to pretend everything is okay.

But it's not, and I can't stop thinking about the danger Grace warned me about.

CHAPTER 18

I've lost January again.

Well, not really lost her, but after last night—sleeping next to her and waking up with her—having her retreat back into her fear, even the tiniest bit, feels like a massive retreat.

We're in my dining room, having finished the food a chef I hired for the night cooked in my kitchen. I've got state-of-the-art everything there, not that I ever cook myself. But it allows me to eat amazing home-cooked meals without lifting a finger.

"You sure everything's okay?" I ask. I point to her dessert plate. "You've hardly touched your chocolate torte."

She pokes at it with her spoon, regret pulling her brows together. "No, it's fantastic, I'm just…"

Tired is what I expect her to finish with, but she doesn't. Instead, she sets the spoon aside with a sigh. When she lifts her gaze to mine, the vulnerability in her blue eyes staggers me.

"January, honey." I reach across the table for her hand. "Tell me what's wrong so I can fix it."

She doesn't deflect or shutter her gaze. If anything, it becomes more open, harder for me to look at without doing... *something.* But if I don't know what's upsetting her, I can't do anything.

I don't do well doing nothing.

Her lips part, and there's a spark in her eyes, half hope, half wondering, saying *Maybe, could I possibly, trust you?*

My hand tightens on hers. Of course she can. Finally she'll be utterly open, utterly truthful, and I can chase away every last dark thought that plagues her. I want that so badly my every muscle is knotted tight except for the ones holding her hand in mine.

Trust me.

But I must have squeezed a little too tightly, wished a little too hard, because a flicker passes across her face as she reconsiders what she was about to say.

Son of a bitch. But I bite that back.

"I'm still in charge, right?" Her swallow is hard enough to clench my heart. "You and the Bastards own part of it, but Ultra is still mine, isn't it?"

I bring her knuckles to my lips and am rewarded with her silky shiver. "Of course. No one's taking anything from you."

If anything, I've been gentler with January than any other founder I've worked with. I've been known to force people out, to require certain hires, even to bring in entirely new management, all the better to get my money's worth.

But January has nothing to worry about. Her team is top-notch, and she runs it well. The things I'm bringing in are only to make it better.

"When it comes time to sell, I won't be forced into anything?"

That she's made that a question kills me. "No. There won't be any forcing of anything." I study her expression, which is still tight. "I'm here to help you, not force you."

The tip of her tongue slips out to wet her lips, and my thoughts scramble for a moment.

"I don't feel forced," she says finally. "But there are certain places I don't want to work."

"Like where?"

She's got very specific names in mind—I can tell by the twitch of her eyelids.

"It's not the places themselves," she says. "I only want to know that I'm not losing control here."

She is and so am I, but not in the way she's thinking. "I'm not taking your baby away from you. Can we make a deal?" I smile, trying to reassure her. "You worry about the encryption, and I'll worry about the deal. That's my specialty. And you still own the majority of shares. Nothing happens without your approval."

Her nod is soft, slow. Finally I'm getting through to her. "You're right. I should finish the system first, then worry about those things."

"Don't worry about those things." I rub her knuckles and down her fingers, trying to push away her worries. "In any deal I make, you'll be my first consideration. Let me do what I do best."

My *main* consideration, I realize with a start. I don't care so much about getting a return on my investment as making sure January gets everything she ever wanted out of this deal.

No one can ever know though—it'd be hell for my reputation.

"Okay." Her smile is brave and fond all at once as she reaches across the table to cup my cheek.

Jesus, the tenderness in her touch makes me want to melt into her. And I don't melt. I can't, because I have to keep her safe.

"This is all so new," she says, caressing my cheekbone. "I'm trying to figure out what it all means."

That does make me melt, or at least my heart does. "Me too," I confess.

I reach into my jacket, which is hanging off the back of my chair, and pull out the velvet box I'd been holding safe for her. For this very perfect moment.

She peers at it with a hint of suspicion, like she can't really believe that box holds what she thinks it does. "What is that?"

"A little congratulation gift."

She sniffs as she opens it slowly. "*Little?* Maybe in size only." When the lid snaps all the way open, her gasp warms me from the inside out.

Inside is a diamond tennis bracelet and matching earrings. It's not ostentatious since I want her to be able to wear them always, but the diamonds are the highest grade, and they're nestled in a soft rose gold setting. Yellow gold would have been too harsh for her pale skin and platinum too cold, but this gold is perfect.

I can see the sparkle of the diamonds in her eyes, along with her happy shock.

"I can take it back," I say when she still hasn't spoken.

She snatches them to her chest with a mock snarl. "Don't you dare." Uncertainty creeps in. "But... but why? They're almost too fancy to wear."

"Nonsense." I rise, then gently pry the box out of her hand. The bracelet slips around her wrist as if made just for her, which it is. "You deserve these."

She holds her wrist close to her heart, admiring the gleam of the jewelry. I take the opportunity to slip one of the earrings in, her earlobe as soft as anything. Something so tender shouldn't be able to hold the cold weight of these earrings, but it does, easily. And in a few moments, her skin will warm the metal.

"I really haven't done anything." But she tilts her head so I can put in the other earring.

When I'm done, I lean back to admire her. Just as I'd

planned, the diamonds are perfect for her, enhancing her beauty rather than overwhelming it. And since she can wear it everywhere, a reminder of me will be with her always.

"How do I look?" She reaches up a single fingertip to touch one of the diamonds in her ears.

"Gorgeous." I pull her up from her chair and swing her up into my arms. "I want you to wear them for me tonight. Those and nothing else."

She answers me with a kiss, deep and needy but also thankful.

I answer her back exactly the same as I carry her off to my bed.

CHAPTER 19

January

I was this close to telling Mark the entire truth last night, and all day I've been second-guessing myself.

I touch one of my earrings, the polished surface of the diamond and the skin-warmed gold calming me. I'm vibrating out of my skin today, what with twenty-four hours between me and Grace's message.

Keep quiet. Keep the evidence hidden.

Too damn late for that. I've gone and built an entire encryption system out of what Grace gave me. Which I probably should tell Mark about at some point.

Scratch that—I have to tell Mark about it, before we get into serious talks about selling Ultra. He said that I would be his first consideration in any deal. Which means he'd be willing to listen to my objections to selling to Corvus if they offer.

Only, how would I make him believe me? I could show him the documents Grace sent, but she said to keep it hidden. How much more danger would she be in if Mark knew?

If I told him, I could put some of this strain and worry

onto Mark's shoulders instead of carrying it all on my own. He's strong enough to take it. Based on what he said last night, I believe he wants to take it.

He wants to be on my side. I simply have to take those last few steps and trust him completely. I want to, but...

I sigh and try to focus. There really is no time today for me to get wrapped up in this. We've finished a ton of testing overnight, and now I'm going line by line through code, tweaking here and debugging there. My team is counting on me to do this today and do it right, and I can't let them down.

Mark is coming by to discuss the test results too. I've already got half a list of the items we need to talk about, and I add another note every few lines of code.

Every second my mind isn't occupied with the task, it darts off into anxiety land, taking dark paths into the forest of *holy fuck, what have I done?*

And then I pull it back into the code for a while before it takes off again.

I grab the paper cup of coffee on my desk and take a long sip. It's three in the afternoon, and that's cup number six for me. Sleep isn't happening tonight.

Thank God I know Mark will have just the ticket for relaxing me. It worked last night, but once I came down off the high of three orgasms in a row, I felt guilty for forgetting my troubles while he was working me over, making me forget my own damn name.

And yet I need him as much as I need to finish this code or this entire encryption system. Everything in my life—him, the company, Grace—is getting bound together in an unbreakable way.

Awesome job, January. I thought you were going to keep things simple?

I write down yet another thing to bring up with Mark

and tell myself to shut up. Things were never going to be simple with him.

When the front door opens, I almost don't jump out of my seat. If I weren't high enough on caffeine that I could see my nerves sparking behind my eyes, I probably wouldn't have.

As it is, I'm shaking before Mark even walks in.

"Great news." He claps his hands as he comes toward my cubicle. Everyone in Ultra is smiling, because Mark only ever brings good things. And if he has great news…

Somehow I can't make myself buy it. Something feels off.

There's a woman behind him, wearing a thin, superior smile. She's dressed like a corporate shark, briefcase in hand, makeup and jewelry just understated enough to let you know that yes, she *is* that effortlessly stylish.

I immediately want to kick her out. She's not here for anything good, no matter what Mark says.

Instead, I rise and walk out, a fake polite smile on my lips. Thank God the clothes Mark ordered for me today are structured and sharp. Warrior garb for a twenty-first-century shield maiden.

"Hi." I reach out a hand to the woman. "I'm January Harris, the founder of Ultra."

The woman's gaze flicks over my hand before she takes it. "Minerva Dyne. Corvus Technologies."

She doesn't say what she does for Corvus, but the name alone is enough to give me chills.

Fuchs's found out about… something. Maybe the documents Grace passed to me or the messaging app I sent her. Or even worse, our messages.

I brace myself for something awful.

What I get is even worse than that.

"On behalf of Corvus, I'm pleased to offer one point five billion for the acquisition of Ultra."

That number is a punch to my gut. No, it's like a full-body blow, knocking the wind right out of me and shorting my brain.

The woman pulls the contracts out from her briefcase, thick and pristine. "We're happy to let your lawyer look things over, but we're also ready to sign today."

This is too fast. Grace messaged me just yesterday, and they're offering this much for the company today?

Fuchs knows what I'm up to, and he's decided that a billion dollars is worth silencing me forever. He's going to buy the company—which means he owns all my intellectual property too—and then he'll quietly sink my encryption program, the same as he's doing to everyone else. If he owns it, he gets to kill it.

It's truly brilliant to bring this offer before the Bastards. I'd counted on him keeping things quiet, as he likes, but he's outmaneuvered me here. The Bastards don't care if my encryption ever sees the light of day—they only want to make money on their investment. The sooner, the better. Fuchs is offering them the quickest, easiest money they've ever made.

I have to slow this down, make it not easy. My thoughts and heart are frantic as I search for any kind of excuse...

"This is... unexpected," I say, which is the understatement of the year. "We haven't even had any initial talks."

Usually a company and a start-up will circle each other for a while, feeling each other out. And the start-up will call a few other companies, let them know a sale is in the air, the better to start a bidding war.

"Apparently when Arne makes up his mind, it's made up," Mark says. He's smiling like Arne is an old friend and isn't this kind of thing just like him?

Stupid me for not telling Mark exactly what old *Arne* is

like before this. I scramble for some other response to Minerva than *The answer is hell no.*

"Our lawyer," I say too quickly. "It will take him some time to go through all this."

Maybe I can have him take forever, and we can have something to sell to Pixio in the meantime. Although they'll have to offer more than a billion dollars for it...

Jesus, I'm in deep shit here.

"Good news." Mark is still smiling like he has no idea I'm freaking out. But why would I be? This is great news. A normal founder would be over the moon about this. "Elliot is heading over, and he'll do an initial read-through right here." He glances over at the door. "And here he is now."

Fuck and double fuck. I sigh inwardly, then look out over my team. "Can everyone take a coffee break? A long one?"

We'll need privacy for this, and there's no conference room in our office. So I've got to kick my poor team out.

Everyone rises and heads for the door, still smiling. Except for Doc. When she catches my eye, she mouths, *What the hell?*

I give a slight shake of my head. She takes the hint and disappears with the others.

When I face who's left, I'm confronted with Mark's smiling, Elliot's scowling, and Minerva Dyne's smirking. Great. So this is going to be just awesome.

"Let me make some space for us." I point to the longest table we have, then start to clear it.

Mark comes over to help me. "What's wrong?" he asks under his breath.

So he actually noticed. It's a little late now to ask though. "I'm fine," I hiss back. I straighten up. "All ready. Anyone want coffee?"

"I'll get it." Mark saves me from having to play secretary.

When we're all settled, the three of us facing off against

Minerva with our mugs in front of us, Elliot pulls out a slim pair of reading glasses from his front jacket pocket. "The contract, please."

"Of course." Minerva's expression is oddly blank as she passes it over. She could be a robot for all the emotion she's showing.

Maybe she is. Maybe Corvus has finally perfected androids or something.

Or maybe the shock of all this is making me loopy.

Mark is smiling again, because of course he is. Fuchs is his friend, his colleague, not someone to fear. This deal will just be another gold brick in the wall of Bastard Capital's reputation.

He'd never understand if I refuse this offer. Not without my spilling all my secrets.

The rustling of the paper as Elliot does his inspection is loud in the silence.

Minerva doesn't look like she wants to pass the time with conversation. Mark, being Mark, tries anyway. "So you're Arne's new assistant? When did you start?"

Her gaze doesn't warm even a single degree as it flicks over him. "Three months ago."

"Is George still with Corvus then?"

"No."

She doesn't say anything else. Mark's smile drops, and I can tell he's struggling not to turn into bad cop.

Thankfully, Elliot pushes the contract away then, and he doesn't look happy. Maybe he can save me from having to say no by refusing her right now on some technicality.

"How long have you been planning this offer?" he says. "You must have drawn this up before Bastard Capital invested."

She makes a slight, dismissive noise. "Our lawyers drew it up after. Not everyone has trouble writing contracts."

Elliot actually flinches. Then he turns a shade of red that clashes horribly with his gray tweed. "I certainly don't. The only trouble anyone has is if they try to break one of my contracts."

"Oh, your reputation is supposed to precede you?" She says it as coolly as she does everything else, so some might miss the bite in it.

But Elliot doesn't. It's clear that after only a few minutes' acquaintance, he loathes this woman.

I don't like her much myself. Anyone who does Fuchs's dirty work has to be a bad person, lacking in moral fiber.

"It's not supposed to," Elliot says. "It does."

A smile, hard and unkind, twitches at the edge of her mouth. "Is everything in order then?" She pulls the contract back to her, already anticipating his answer.

Elliot pulls it back. "No. I'll need more time to review this, and Ultra's lawyer will have to as well. Send me an electronic copy as soon as you can." He pauses a bare moment. "Which you should have done before this meeting. It's almost like you're trying to get away with something here."

She actually, *actually* blushes. Not anything major, just a spot of pink in her cheeks, but it's enough to floor me. Finally a human reaction from the ice queen.

And *Go, Elliot.* If he's suspicious about this whole thing, so much the better.

"Fine." Minerva rises, her expression blank as blank can be again. "I'll email you." She heads for the door, then stops halfway. "Oh, and one more thing. There's a time limit on that offer. One week to say yes. Or we withdraw the deal."

With that last twist of the knife, she's gone. I can only stare after her for long moments, trying to breathe.

I am beyond fucked now.

"January." Mark is holding my arm, trying to get my attention. "What the hell is going on?"

I stand up, ignoring Elliot, and grab Mark's hand. Then I'm dragging him out of the office and into the hallway while he splutters with shock.

Well, he'll just have to get used to it. Because I'm about to tell him all my secrets. Even the most shocking ones.

CHAPTER 20

Something has snapped in January.

I'm not sure what it was about Fuchs's offer—or his cold assistant—that set her off, and I hardly have time to ask her as she drags me down the hall. Besides, I don't want her to stop whatever she's doing.

My gut tells me she's finally going to reveal whatever dark thing has been driving her all this time. And my gut is rarely wrong.

She stops by the elevators, looking frantically around us. But there's no one there.

"January, stop."

Her eyes are too wide, searching, searching.

"Honey, listen to me. Just take a breath."

She does, and as the oxygen hits her brain, some of the panic leaves her. "I can't do this," she whispers, as if afraid of being overheard.

"You won't have to work for Corvus. None of you will." I can make that deal for her, easy. "The money they're offering here… you can do whatever you want with it."

All right, so she's opposed to Corvus for some reason, but that much money ought to overcome any objections.

"You don't understand. And I can't explain where we might be heard."

"January—"

She lays her finger over my lips. I take the opportunity to kiss it. Light flares in her gaze, brief and bright, but then it's gone.

She reaches into my pocket, her fingers groping along my thigh, and she comes out with my phone. The phone clicks sharply as she sets it on the table in the hall, right next to the fake-flower arrangement there, and then she's pulling me along again.

There's only a few other companies on this floor, and none of them have anything to do with encryption. So where are we going?

The stairwell, that's where. I try not to think of my poor, abandoned phone sitting there all by its lonesome as she and I pound down the stairs. We come out on the first floor, and she ducks into a dimly lit hallway, one with only a single door in it.

The door is labeled UTILITY CLOSET, and she opens it and slips us both inside quick as can be.

There's utter darkness for a moment, our breathing the only sign of life until I reach up and pull on the one bare bulb.

January blinks against the sudden light. And keeps blinking like she's about to cry. So I pull her into my arms.

"What's wrong?" I say into her hair. "Tell me, and I'll fix it. I'll fix anything for you."

She's holding tight to my shirt as she buries her face into my chest. She seems so small, smells so innocent, like soap and flowers. Who would want to scare her like this?

And why would it be Fuchs's offer? That's a dream amount of money.

She finally lifts her head and puts her mouth against my ear. "He has cameras and microphones everywhere."

I whisper back, even though I don't understand the need for all this. "Who?"

"Fuchs. He has a spyware app."

My shoulders sag with relief. "That's who's got you spooked. Honey, you shouldn't believe all the tinfoil-hat stuff about him."

Some news sources talk about Fuchs like he's some kind of Bond supervillain instead of what he really is—an awkward tech geek who's paranoid about privacy but not any weirder than anyone else in the valley.

"It's not tinfoil-hat. I have proof."

My instinct is to not believe her. I've had drinks with Fuchs, chatted with him about the industry. Okay, so he's more secretive than most, but that doesn't make him a villain with a secret plan.

But January isn't a crackpot. Whatever proof she has is enough to scare her, which means I have to listen to her in good faith even if I don't buy it.

I take her face in my hands. "Tell me. And know that no matter what, I'll keep you safe."

That's what starts her crying, and the sight of the tears running down her cheeks makes my gut want to tear in half.

"You can't," she gets out between sobs. "You don't know how powerful he is."

As for power, he's got no more than the CEO of any other tech company, and she's not here crying to me about Jack from Pixio. He's got his phones in the hands of half the world, which seems better for world domination than some piddling spyware.

She's underestimating me and the Bastards, but I let it slide. "Then tell me."

"I had a friend, Grace. She was my roommate."

Had makes chills run down my spine. But Fuchs's no murderer. There's no way.

"She works for Corvus. About six months ago, she had to move into company housing. And everything of hers went dark. Email, Twitter, Facebook, even her phone. I was so worried, but I had no way to contact her."

"Wait, was she kidnapped? Then we definitely have to call the police." And what the hell does this have to do with Corvus's alleged spyware?

January shakes her head. "She's not a citizen—she's here on an H-1. So if her employer wants her to move to 'secure housing,' only use a company phone... how can she really say no? If they fire her, she's out of the country. Fuchs hires a lot of H-1s, probably so he can control them more easily."

And also because they're cheaper than hiring citizens. CEOs make a lot of noise about how we don't have enough homegrown talent here in the US, but it's not true—they just want cheap labor. Everything else she's described—a company phone, company housing, rules about social media —isn't unusual either.

"Okay, so you think she's in Corvus housing. And is still working for them. Where does the spyware come in?"

I try to keep the skepticism out of that but don't succeed. January catches that and stiffens in my arms.

"I'm not lying."

"I didn't say you were."

"But you don't believe me." She shifts like she's going to break away from me.

I tighten my arms around her and try to think of something to say, something that will reassure her.

How am I supposed to answer that? Her friend disappeared but not really. As far as January knows, Grace just doesn't want to be contacted, which isn't a crime.

Her mouth twists when I don't respond. "Last July there

was a document in my secure shared file. No indication of where or who it was from, but it was named something only Grace would use. And inside were all Fuchs's plans. He's got spyware on every phone he can, embedded in social media apps, and he's just waiting to turn it on. Grace is working on it within the company."

That's… that's a little more disturbing. But hardly more believable. "You got these documents out of nowhere, and you believe them? And that they came from her? And even if Corvus has done this"—which I'm doubting—"he can't turn on phone cameras or microphones without legal permission."

Her look is skeptical. "He's put it in the terms of service allowing him to do it. And how many people ever read those when they install an app?"

I turn that over in my mind. No one reads that stuff, but still, putting spyware to activate the phone without permission? Someone would have known what Corvus was up to, would have blown the whistle before now.

With an angry huff, January grabs my hand. "I can see you still don't believe me. Well, fine, I can prove it to you. *Really* prove it."

She drags me back to her desk, never once speaking. I try to get a word in somewhere between the stairwell and the Ultra office—and try to grab my phone back—but she silences me with a fierce look.

"He's listening," she snaps.

I know he's not, but I stay quiet anyway. Maybe January is cracking under all this pressure and she's projecting her anxieties onto Fuchs.

Or maybe I can't let myself believe that Fuchs would do something like that.

When we get to her cubicle, she pulls a laptop out of a drawer, along with a partially disassembled phone. With a few clicks, she's got the laptop up and running.

The phone is dead, the screen black, and when January taps at the screen, nothing happens. She holds it before me, her expression imploring.

I nod when I get it. The phone is off, completely powered down. She wants to make certain I can see that.

She props it up so that the back camera is facing a photo she's pinned to the cubicle wall, one of the entire Ultra team at the polo fields in Golden Gate Park.

I cross my arms and wait, but a frisson of ice climbs up my spine. She's deadly serious about this. Which means...

I try not to remember my own phone, all the things someone might have recorded me doing, all without my knowledge or consent.

Once she's pulled up a command window, she taps hard on the screen at the code, then reaches for a pad and a pen.

I pulled this code out of the PopPix app, she writes.

PopPix is the app everyone uses to share photos, selfies, lunches, coffees, and other tiny details of life, along with comments. Of course PopPix has to access your phone camera—the app wouldn't work without it—but it shouldn't be controlling the camera when the app's not active and especially not when the phone is off.

When January begins to type in commands, the hair on the back of my neck rises, although nothing is happening. A window pops up on the laptop screen, black as the phone screen.

And then the photo appears, the entire Ultra team smiling back at me from the laptop screen, just as they are from the cubicle wall.

The phone hasn't turned on. I tap the screen, hit the home button. Nothing. The phone is as dead as ever.

Except the camera is on, clearly, and taking images. Now that I've moved the phone, the papers on her desk are up on the laptop screen, captured at the phone camera's command.

When I toss the phone down, it hits with a sharp clatter, the only noise either one of us has made for several minutes.

Data on the phone is *supposed* to be encrypted, along with the phone itself, locked with a passcode or a thumbprint. Somehow Fuchs has gotten around both of those safeguards.

Son of a bitch. Fuchs came to our parties, shook our hands, wanted to do deals with us... and he's planning on peeping into our windows like some kind of sicko.

I want to puke and punch him in the jaw all at the same time. My fists flex, imagining him beneath them, being punished as he deserves.

January catches my eye, her expression sadly resigned. She didn't want to have to be right about this.

This time I drag her down to the supply closet, giving my poor phone a hard glare as we pass. I don't even think about picking it up.

When I slam the door closed, I pull her into my arms. "I'm sorry," I whisper into her hair. "I wish I could have believed right away."

If I could have gone back and erased all my skepticism... but it's too late for that. I can only do my best to keep her safe now.

"I know why you couldn't." The forgiveness there hits me right in the chest.

"You'll have to show me all the documents Grace sent you. The fact that she committed corporate espionage like that... It makes things more difficult."

The things I'm referring to is stopping Fuchs and grinding his company into the dust. I'm remembering everything I've ever heard about Corvus, and it's all beginning to make a certain horrible sense. Corvus specializes in surveillance, whether it's for police departments, state intelligence agencies, or even foreign governments. And what better way to watch people, all the people, than through their phones?

It also explains why Fuchs's been buying up encryption companies. He's not interested in protecting data—he wants to make sure it's entirely exposed to his all-seeing eyes.

I'm pissed at him, but I'm also pissed at myself for missing all this. I've seen him around, chatted with him—I'm supposed to be good at reading people, but I've completely fucked it up with him.

"I think Grace felt like she didn't have any other choice," January says. She sags against me, but it's more from exhaustion than relief. "I've been working so hard for so long on this encryption system, and now he comes in with this ridiculous offer. Everyone's going to think I'm crazy for turning it down. And Fuchs will suspect something as soon as I do." She goes stiff under my arm. "And the other Bastards? How are you going to explain this to them? You can't put Grace in danger by telling them."

Those men are my brothers; I could trust them with anything. But January can't, at least not yet.

"Can I at least tell Dev? We're going to need some backup here. And he's as silent as the grave."

Dev's going to be furious when he hears about this. All the Bastards will, but him most of all. Privacy is beyond an obsession with him.

January swallows hard, but she doesn't immediately say no. "What can you even do?"

I can think of several things, mostly involving my jacking up Fuchs. But that's not how we solve things here. Besides, physical pain is fleeting, and I want Fuchs to hurt for a very long time.

"First we finish the encryption system. The sooner it's

running in smartphones, the better. We've got a secure location we can move your team to."

January doesn't know it yet, but she's not going with them. I need her someplace even more secure, somewhere I know Fuchs would never dare to trespass. She can manage her team remotely. And I can make sure she's safe twenty-four seven.

"And Grace?" she says. "I can't leave her where she is. She's risked a lot to send me those documents."

Which I'll need to see ASAP. I trust January's story completely now, but I want to get a look for myself. As for Grace...

My jaw clenches as January stares up at me, eyes dark and wide with appeal. She's desperate for me to save her friend. God, I wish there was an easy way to buy us out of this situation.

"She could always quit," I say. If she's truly in danger, it might be for the best. "She'd have to go back to..."

"China," January supplies. "But she doesn't want to. Getting an H-1B is so hard, and she'll get a green card at the end. If she quits, she'll never get another chance like this."

January's right, and I can't see any path forward that ends happily for her friend.

I set my chin on her hair. Even though the closet smells of bleach, the scent of her shampoo still reaches me. Her chest rises and falls, brushing against mine. Somehow the shabbiness of our surroundings makes the moment even more intimate.

"We'll figure something out," I say. Grace going to another company will be tricky, especially with what she knows about Corvus. Fuchs isn't going to simply let her walk away. "Elliot knows a ton of immigration lawyers. This must have happened before."

The tiniest of laughs escapes her. "I do know one person

who got to stay after their H-1B was terminated. They had to marry a citizen."

The coil of tension in my spine loosens at her amusement. "Okay, I'll put find a likely spouse on my to-do list. What's her type?"

Another laugh from her, which warms me all over. If she can laugh, then everything will be okay. I'll spend every dime I have, twist the arm of every contact I have, to fix this for her. I need her to know that.

"You could've told me," I say.

She goes very still, only her breath moving between us. "No, I couldn't. I didn't know if you were friendly with him, and when Grace disappeared and then sent me those files... I was so frightened. I *am* so frightened."

"No." I tighten my arms, pulling her closer. "You have nothing to fear anymore. Fuchs may be an asshole, but so am I."

Her asshole.

When she turns her face up to mine, the blue of her eyes is stark even in the bare light from the dinky bulb. "So you're on my side?"

I brush my lips over her temple, the pulse there like butterfly wings. "Yes. Always."

Her shudder is one of relief. "But what about the money? You invested so much—"

"I don't give a shit about the money." For once, I truly don't. "All I care about is your safety."

My heart wants to jump out of my chest. This is the worst possible time to realize that I'm falling hard for January, but I have to tell her the truth. She really is all I care about right now.

She nods. "Okay. I... I trust you." She blinks as if clearing her head. "I guess I'd better get to packing up the office. Can I let everyone know where we're going?"

I shake my head. I'm willing to tell the Bastards, but her team doesn't need to know the rest. They'll be safer that way. "All they need to know is that they're going to a new building. A more secure one. Everything else is too sensitive to share."

We'll tell her team there's a rival company trying to beat them to market and that we need to move fast if we want to sell to Pixio. It's a common enough story they'll believe without question. And they'll work their asses off without question too.

"Wait." She puts a few inches between us as she realizes. "*They?* Not me?"

"No. We're going somewhere Fuchs can't get to you."

Even our secure building is too close to the belly of the beast for my comfort. Fuchs wants her, but I'm never letting him have her. Not even a glimpse.

"Where, Antarctica?" she asks.

"That's a bit farther than I had in mind. And colder." I can't help but smile, because she's way off track here.

She raises her eyebrows. "So where?"

"Napa."

When her mouth drops open, I take advantage and steal a kiss.

Once we're up in Wine Country, safe from Fuchs's prying eyes, we'll have time for more. But I'm greedy.

For her. And only her suddenly.

CHAPTER 21

January

Even though I'm technically on the run from one of the most powerful, secretive men in the tech world—oh, and racing against the clock to stop his evil plans—the sight of the winery rising before us, waiting like a castle at the end of a fairy tale, makes me gasp with delight.

"Of course you own a winery," I say.

Mark turns the Tesla into the main driveway. "It's not mine. It's Logan's."

I insisted that we stay in the City long enough for me to see my team safely to the secure building, although Mark wanted to drag me off to Napa straight from the janitor's closet.

My team surprisingly took the news without many questions. Mark simply said that he'd arranged for better office spaces for us, and they went along with it. They didn't even say anything when he told them I'd be working off-site with him.

Mark also arranged for someone to get my clothes from my apartment and explain my absence to my roommates, dealt with the lease on our current office space, conferred with the other Bastards about what to do after bringing them into the loop, and never once let me out of his sight.

I don't know what he has planned beyond selling the Ultra system to Pixio, but I trust that whatever it is, it will work.

We come to a stop in front of the house. It's done in a French château style, the roof dark gray slate and the windows set with cut leaded glass. The afternoon sun paints it and the green vines snaking up the rolling hills in a wash of gold. I expect Cinderella or Sleeping Beauty to step out at any moment, a long-stemmed glass of red wine in her hand.

"This is Logan's?" I ask as Mark comes around to open my door. "How often does he come here?"

Logan might look like Prince Charming, but I find it hard to picture him in this "house."

"Hardly ever." Mark hands me out of the car. "He bought it for Callie. And then she left him."

I walk up to the massive oaken door, trying to get my mouth to close. "She left him right after he bought her a winery?"

Mark shrugs as he unlocks the door. "I don't think the two are related, though she never told him why she was leaving."

The entry foyer is almost as impressive as the exterior. Marble tiles veined with various shades of red, white, and gold are set in a complicated pattern beneath our feet. The ceiling rises two stories above our head, and the floor-to-ceiling windows illuminate the double staircase at the end of the hall.

"I can't imagine anyone not liking this. Is there someone who at least takes care of the vines?"

Mark shuts the front door with a weighty, echoing thunk. "There's a management company for the vineyard. And someone comes in every other week to air things out. But otherwise, no one's going to disturb us."

"So no interruptions while we work?" It's a relief to hear but also exciting. Yeah, I need to work my butt off and keep up with what my team is doing, but we're in a freaking castle, just the two of us, for probably weeks.

Mark's smile is knowing. "Nope, not a one. We've got a secure internet connection once we get it set up. But with our phones off, we should be unreachable."

That was the other thing Mark did before we left—turned off both his phone and mine and got my entire team brand-new work phones. He told my employees to leave their personal phones at home and to never discuss the project outside our new secure building. Again, they accepted it pretty readily. Getting rid of any and all phones entirely would have been best, but my team definitely would have said something about that. And we can't explain to them the real reason for all this cloak-and-dagger stuff.

"I left my phone at your place." I walk across the marble floor, peeking into the rooms opening into the foyer. One is the living room—or maybe something that fancy is a parlor?—done in shades of burnt orange and bright golds, the same as a brilliant sunset. A huge swath of the vineyard is visible through the windows. "So I'd say I'm pretty secure."

Mark pats his pocket. "And I've got a burner." He looks around. "Do you want the tour?"

I do, but... "Let's get our work area set up. We can do the tour when I'm too exhausted to think anymore."

Mark raises an eyebrow. "Among other things."

Two hours later, I'm beginning to see the cracks in Mark's oh-so-perfect façade. He's typing away at a terminal screen, his fingers somewhat hesitant. Like he's forgotten what he's doing.

"No," I say as the string he's typing comes up. "Do you not remember this?"

We're trying to get the internet set up, but like all things technical, it's taking us longer than we'd hoped. Even programmers sometimes shake their fists at the idiot machines they have to work with.

"No, I remember." Frustration leaks out of his voice. I'm reminded of the times together in the computer lab at Stanford, when we'd both be working on some assignment and he'd grumble about it in that exact same tone. His fingers start again.

"No," I say again. This time I push his hands aside, and Mr. Master of Silicon Valley lets me. "Let me do it. Wow, you really have forgotten stuff."

When I hit Enter, the screen flashes as data packets go flying between Mark's laptop and the website we're pinging. Finally something's working.

"I haven't forgotten," Mark says, but his lower lip is adorably pouty. "It's like riding a bike."

"Right." I tap in some more commands, double-checking the connection. "Except a bike is pretty much the same as it's always been and code changes constantly."

When I look up from the screen, he's smiling at me, all fond and warm.

"You're enjoying this, aren't you?"

Okay, maybe I am. I shrug. "It's strange to be better than you at something for once."

"Wait, what?" He grabs me and pulls me down into his lap. "You always got better grades than I did."

I love that he does this now, just pulls me into him for a cuddle—or more—whenever the mood takes him. Out there, he's the lion, taking down lesser foes and ruling the plains. But here, with me, he's my kitten. Or maybe I'm his.

"Yes," I say, "but I worked ten times as hard. It always

seemed to come so effortlessly to you. Like you were born knowing how to code and I was running as fast as I could just to stay in the same place."

I might have gotten the grades, but he was the one who'd made it big. In a world where people proudly proclaimed their dropout status alongside their bank balances, he's the winner, not me.

"That's not how it was at all. I wasn't naturally better—I was lazier."

I snort. He was no such thing. "Okay, lazier, but also better. If you had worked as hard as I did, you would have smoked me."

"Is that really what you believe? That you have no natural talent and I do?" His hand is stroking my back, long, gentle strokes, but his body has gone tense.

"Well, I have some natural talent." I shake my head. "But I'm not some boy-wonder coder. Hard work isn't sexy here—flashes of genius are."

I'm only speaking the truth, and he knows it. Programmers who keep their heads down and get stuff done are appreciated... but they're not celebrated. And I've always been the head-down type.

"Your encryption program is genius." I can't see his expression, but the conviction in his tone rattles through me. "Honest-to-God, once-in-a-lifetime genius."

Of course it feels wonderful to hear that, so much so that I've got a massive lump in my throat. But some perverse part of me wants to push back, to downplay what I've done.

"You said it yourself," I point out. "Who needs that much encryption on their personal pictures?"

I know that it's necessary. I know that I'm right... but all my vulnerabilities are spilling out, into the safety of his hearing.

"But you proved I was wrong."

I melt into warmth and happiness, finally able to believe. "Wait." I put a hand to my ear, suddenly giddy. "What was that I heard?"

He gives an irritated rumble. "You're annoying, you know that?"

I tilt my head to grin up at him. "Only sixty-seven percent of the time."

"You can't use my own jokes against me. That's a violation of joke law."

"Let's go back to what you said before then."

His sigh is heavy, but his eyes are twinkling. "I was wrong. It happens sometimes. But not often."

"Of course not."

His expression turns serious. "January, once this is out there, you'll be able to do anything you want. You'll be that famous."

"I don't want to be famous. I think... Well, I think running Ultra is what I really want to do. I don't want to jump ship for something better. For me, there is nothing better."

"And you'll be able to do that. But there's nothing else?"

Dream big, is what he's saying. Only, if Ultra is on steady ground and we're together, I can't imagine what else I might ask from life. "There is something," I say. "But it's kind of silly."

"I like silly."

He doesn't, actually. He's funny and charming and devastatingly sexy, but he's not anywhere near silly. I'm amazed he even uses the word, he's so far from it.

"There's this guy on the internet who makes Enigmas. Reproductions of the original German code machines," I explain. "He machines and hand assembles each one."

I saw one once at an encryption conference. Another historical enthusiast had one out to show the other attendees. I'd coveted it like nothing else in my life, but when he told me the price, I knew I'd have to hit it big or sell a kidney to afford one. And since I was still living with roommates and both my kidneys, the dream of having one was far, far away.

"That sounds amazing," Mark says. "Does he sell plans?"

"Like, to make your own? Yeah, but you'd need a high-end machine shop. Which I don't have."

He's quiet for several long moments, his expression unreadable. And then he kisses me, making forget everything but him. I pull him close, greedy for him, but then the computer chimes.

Work. I really do have to work.

Mark sighs, then spins me around in his lap so I'm facing the computer. "Someday your Ultra will be world famous. And then you can get the old-fashioned encryption machine you've always wanted."

"But first," I say, staring at the command window as it waits for me to pour code into it, "I have to finish it."

Mark puts his mouth against my ear. "I know you can."

So I start typing.

CHAPTER 22

January

We've reached the point in the day where my brain has turned to mush.

Even though Mark still looks fresh as ever, after twelve solid hours of coding, checking in with the team, and going over the chip-testing results, I'm ready to pop something in the microwave, then collapse on the couch for several hours of fitful sleep. Except that in this magical place, I get to eat a lovely, hot meal prepared by the chef Mark has hired and to lounge on the back patio, watching the sun go down with a glass of wine in my hand.

It turns out that Logan sells his grapes to one of the most exclusive boutique wineries in Napa. I'm drinking a wine that most people have to go on a wait list for and then pay hundreds of dollars for one measly bottle. Mark, however, opened a wine cellar filled to the ceiling with bottles and popped one open.

I turn the wineglass in my hand, let the light tangle in it. This place is almost too magical to be real, with the sunshine pouring in and the scent of rich earth and ripe grapes filling the air. One level below us, built into the cliffside, the spa bubbles and burbles, waiting for us to soak away the cares of the day. It's physically impossible for me to be stressed here, which has made my work go all the faster. I've become a lean, mean coding machine. And my team is doing the same at the secure site. We're three days into this, and I'm certain that in three weeks or less, we'll be ready to pitch to Pixio.

For the first time in a long time, I have hope. This system is going to be done soon, and it will be so amazing Pixio will have to buy it. And while Mark hasn't told me much, I know he's pulling strings in the background, making calls, cashing in favors, and finding a team of immigration lawyers.

Oh, and taking care of me as I code my brains out. Turns out that hours of sweaty, mind-blowing sex is almost as restorative as sleep.

I look over at him sitting on the lounge chair next to me. Sometimes it's hard to believe this is the same guy I knew in college. He's so confident, so powerful, it radiates from him. And then he'll smile, a real one, and it's like we're transported back five years.

He catches me looking. "Everything okay? Do you need anything?"

I shake my head. Good food, good wine, beautiful view—what more could I possibly want?

Except there is something more that I want. "What did you do after college?" I ask. "I mean really. I've read the magazine profiles, but none of them sound like you. Like the Mark I remember."

"It's not that interesting. I knew from the beginning I never wanted to work for anyone else. Google, Pixio, Face-book—they all made me offers, but I turned them down."

A ton of people would give a kidney to work at those places, but he had to be independent, even right out of school. I respect that—I didn't even bother applying at any big places myself. I picked a tiny start-up with tech I believed in instead.

"What did you want to do?" I ask.

Mark laughs. "Whatever I wanted, although I still wasn't quite sure what that might be. But no one was going to give me a million dollars to do that fresh out of college, so I did some freelance coding for a while. Nothing major but enough to live on. Paul and I were roommates by then, and we invited Logan to come live with us too."

"Paul had a roommate?" He could have afforded any house in Palo Alto he wanted. A ten bedroom could have been all his to rattle around in.

"Paul actually likes to live as close to what he calls normal as possible. It's one of his quirks."

I guess when you're born rich, you can afford any quirks you want. "Okay, so you're all living like slobs, coding by night and gaming by day. Then what?"

"The house was... cleanish." Mark's forehead furrows. "Like eighty-five percent clean."

"You definitely made up that statistic. How did Finn and Dev come in?"

"Finn ended up crashing on our couch for a month while he did a contract job up here. And then he just ended up staying. We were talking about code and hardware all the time then. We had so many ideas, so many ways we wanted to upend the world."

I can tell from his smile that it was a wonderful time in his life. I can empathize. Those first few months of Ultra, when I was working all hours, frantically trying to get all my ideas out and functioning, were amazing. Exhausting and terrifying but also amazing.

"What happened to all those ideas?" I ask. The stock market predictor was what had made them famous—and rich—but they never sold it. Or anything else. Instead, they went straight from that into the VC world.

"Oh, I've got some still rattling around in my head. Not as

many as before though." His mouth tightens. He doesn't like that.

"And the stock market predictor? You guys never did anything more with that."

It remains one of the great mysteries of the valley. Who had that code? Were they still using it to make money on Wall Street?

Mark takes a hesitant breath. "I'll tell you, but no one else knows. And you can never tell."

I cross my heart. "I'll never breathe a word." But my nerves are humming, because he *trusts* me. Like I trust him.

"When Dev came, everything finally clicked. We became... more than a team." Mark takes a sip of his wine, and I want to shout at him to go on because he's getting to the good part. "But Dev's the one who wrote the initial stock-price algorithm. We all refined it, but without his initial code, it never would have happened."

Well, that's one mystery answered. But considering that it's kind of an open secret at this point—most speculation has already centered on Dev as the brains—I have to ask, "Why can't anyone know?"

"Dev... he doesn't like attention."

I'd gotten that part, but not why. "Is there something in his past?"

Mark shrugs. "Your guess is as good as mine. I don't know anything about his past. I don't know if *Dev* even knows anything about his past. He never talks about family— not parents, siblings, nothing. No childhood memories, nothing about school. He really is a blank slate."

Considering how close the Bastards are, if Dev hasn't said anything about his past, there must be nothing to tell. "And the program? Do you guys still use it to play the market?"

Mark slides me a look. "You'll laugh."

"I won't."

"You will," he assures me. He takes a long sip of his wine. "We deleted it."

"What?" Thank God I don't have a mouthful of wine or else I'd have spewed it on him. "Why would you do that? That program basically printed money."

"Exactly. It was too easy. We decided we were going to take those initial earnings and do something else. Something harder. So we deleted the program."

I fall back into my lounge chair, my mouth hanging open. The arrogance of doing such a thing is beyond me. The Bastards really are a breed apart.

"Holy hell," I whisper.

"Told you." Mark's smugness is both adorable and annoying.

"I didn't laugh." Nope, I'm not anywhere near laughing. I'm stunned. I wanted the whole story, but this was a humdinger. "And what about Anjie?"

She might not be a Bastard, but the past few days have proven how integral she is to them. Mark was on the phone with her almost every hour, working on Ultra stuff and everything else he has going on. She must be talking to at least one of them all hours of the day.

"Mmm, Anjie." Mark's expression is fond, but I don't feel any jealousy. I know by now that Anjie is only a friend. "She actually came into the garage right after we hit it big, before we'd even started to look for a proper office space. She'd read about us in *Disrupt Dispatch*, realized she'd been passing our garage every day on the way to her job, and decided to see if we needed an office manager. The rest is history."

So I wasn't too far off in thinking of Anjie as a fairy godmother. "That's amazing. You're lucky to have her."

"I know. We're all brothers, but Anjie is our glue."

He comes over to my chair, the heat in his eyes setting my skin on fire. I move my legs to give him room. He's got intentions behind that gaze, intentions that promise me the ultimate pleasure.

My breath catches in my throat as he sits next to me, reaching out for my bare leg. Sparks fly in the gap between us. When he makes contact, a thousand nerve ends take flight in my skin. It's such a small part of me that he's touching, but all of me hums in response.

He leans forward, studying my face. I wait for him to kiss me, to slide his hand up my thigh... but Mark holds there, watching me as his hand makes slow, small circles on my calf. It's maddening and arousing all at once.

Our breathing falls into sync, pushing and pulling together. The setting sun is warm, I'm flushed with pleasure and wine, and he's oh so close...

"Why did you turn me down in college?"

My eyes go wide and my skin goes cold as I rear back. That's the very last thing I expect him to say.

Mark doesn't react to my shock, his gaze still hard on mine as his hand softly strokes my leg. I lick my lips, trying to form an answer. "Well, it's..."

I lift a hand, unable to go on. My throat is tight with all the reasons, too many to spill out at once.

"I'm not asking to be a dick," he says. "It's just... your saying no has always lingered with me."

I've marked him then. I didn't mean to, I was only trying to protect myself, but still, I hurt him.

"It wasn't personal." I can at least assure him of that. I take a bracing sip of my wine, trying to clear my throat. "I mean, it *was* personal though. We were friends, real friends." I take another sip, bigger than the last. "And actually, I really, really liked you, but I was afraid."

"Of me?" Now he's shocked. "In college?"

For all Mark's wealth and worldly experience, there's still

so much he doesn't understand. He's been rich in the valley for too long—and has been a man his entire life.

I know what he's not saying: *I'd never hurt a woman.* But like I said before, it wasn't personal.

"Do you remember Chloe?" I ask quietly.

"Chloe?" He remembers her, but he's ashamed that he does. "What about her?"

"How she had to leave... What all those boys said about her... And the pictures plastered all over the web."

The pictures haunted me, things Chloe had never intended anyone to see. Those could never be scrubbed from the internet. And she'd trusted Joe so much, letting him take those pictures. He'd turned them into a weapon against her, punishing her for her supposed crimes against him.

"I remember." Mark's voice is cold. "You thought I could do that to you?"

I swallow hard. I didn't ask if he was involved in what had happened to her. I'm afraid to now.

He saw the pictures, I'm sure. Did he share them with his friends? Did he post hateful things about her online?

I don't want to know. I'm a coward.

"I had to protect myself," I say. "You don't understand."

"From me?"

"From all of you."

There's a heavy moment of silence. I don't know how else to explain it to him, and with his own trust issues, he should see where I'm coming from. People think he should give them money simply because he's rich; well, men think I should give them sex simply because I'm a woman.

His face is a study in chilled outrage, all prickly male honor. This is why I didn't want to say anything. Men always have to make it about themselves.

Then he sighs heavily and rubs at his forehead. "You're right."

I blink. "I am? About... your hurting me?" I don't ask about Chloe.

"No," he says quickly. "I never would have hurt you. But you're right that I don't understand. I've never even considered that what happened to Chloe might be the reason. It's just..." He scrubs his hand through his hair, his biceps taut. "I was so crazy about you. Still am, it turns out."

That's when I open my arms and nestle into him. I turn my face into his chest, overcome. Because I'm crazy about him too. The breeze runs over both of us, rich with the scent of ripening grapes and threaded with the calls of the birds.

Finally my voice starts to work again. "I'm crazy about you too," I whisper. "Always have been."

There. That's the last secret between us.

He kisses my hair, my temple, the tip of my ear, telling me without words that he understands.

We haven't said the *L* word, but it's coming. I can feel it sneaking up on both of us. And when Mark gathers me into his arms and carries me into the bedroom, it comes even closer, right on the thresholds of our hearts.

CHAPTER 23

I've overslept.

When I open my eyes and immediately go to check my phone, I realize that January is in my arms.

And then I realize that the bedside clock reads 8:34. I haven't slept this late since college.

My heart gives a kick, then January snuffles and wriggles closer to me. Everything becomes still and quiet, me most of all.

Peace. That's what this sensation is, I realize. January brings me peace.

She also makes me laugh, makes my blood sing, and I trust her. I'd say I've forgotten what that's like, but no woman has ever made me feel this way. Except her. Always her.

I could blame it on Napa, on being secreted away together in the winery, but I know that's a lie. Because as wonderful as it's been, I don't want to stay here forever with her.

I want to bring her back to my house, my bed, and make it ours.

Christ, I've fallen in love.

I think she has too.

She wakes up then, and her smile is just radiant. My mood instantly lightens at the sight.

And then she stretches and I remember last night, which was anything but light and bright. It was dark and intense and the best sex I've ever had. I frame her face and kiss her good morning, putting some of those memories into it. But before long I have to pull away even though both of us are panting. Sadly, we still have work to get to.

January moans in protest. "We have time for a quickie."

I'm not going to argue with that, especially not when she's straddling me, her gorgeous breasts swaying as she settles into place. I grab a condom from the sleeve on the bedside table, and in two seconds I'm inside her, exactly where I'm meant to be.

I was wrong about last night. *This* is the best sex of my life, with January riding me hard and quick, her cheeks flushed with sleep and her hair a wild tangle. *This* is how I want to wake up every morning, first with her in my arms and then with the two of us entangled together.

I'm chanting her name as I come, and she's chanting mine. I've never had a moment more perfect in my life.

Once we release Ultra and defeat Fuchs, I'm keeping her by my side. Forever.

But first we've got to finish the damn system.

An hour later, we're hard at work in the workspace we've set up in one of the guest rooms. January's decided it's time to do a test run of Ultra. We've got Fuchs's spyware running on a phone we've taken apart, and I'm installing the chip in it. The idea is we'll use Fuchs's spyware to activate the phone's camera and see if Ultra can encrypt the images.

At least that's the idea. She's put me in charge of installing the chip, and it's not going so smoothly. Not that I'm going to ask her for help. I used to do stuff like this in my sleep, and in a few minutes, it will all come back to me—

"Wow, you've gotten so terrible at soldering," January says as she looks over my shoulder. "It's actually cute."

Besides the Bastards, there's no one in my life who'd dare talk to me like that. And I love her for it. "It's not terrible." The connections are sound, if not exactly pretty. "You're the one who wanted me to get back to my roots."

Which she's right about. I'd forgotten how satisfying it is to wire up circuits, to get my hands dirty with hardware.

"I guess you just need some practice," January says, plugging our jerry-rigged phone into her laptop. "Maybe I could get you one of those my-first-electronics kits from a toy store."

I roll my eyes, which makes her giggle. "I know you remember that I always had the highest score on our electronics lab assignments."

She shakes her head as her fingers fly over the keyboard. "Nope, we *tied* for first. It seems that your mind is slipping."

I nip at the spot where her neck meets her shoulder, soft and succulent. When all this is done, I'm flying her to some private island for a month of nothing but relaxation and sex. "We tied in algorithms. And you kicked my ass in compilers."

Her fingers slow as she leans into me. "Yes, I did." She turns her head and gives me a long, drugging kiss. "But you still need to brush up on your soldering."

I'm still laughing when she announces, "It's ready."

The atmosphere in the room is suddenly heavy. I can tell she's nervous, but I'm not at all. I know Ultra will work because she designed it.

I set my hands on her shoulders and squeeze. "It will work. You know it will."

She takes an unsteady breath. "I'll test the spyware first. I definitely know that works."

Seeing the images and sounds being recorded from a phone that was supposed to be powered down, its screen completely black, has haunted me since she demo'd it for me.

I haven't told January because she doesn't need to worry, but the Bastards and I have sworn to bring Fuchs down. He's not getting away with this. And it's personal for me since he went after January.

Soon enough, the entire valley will know she's mine and completely untouchable.

The spyware window pops up then, the screen blank because the camera isn't active. My skin tingles anyway, as if there are eyes on the back of my neck.

January's fingers began to tremble slightly. I kiss her hair, reminding her that she's safe with me.

"Okay," she says softly and hits the Enter key.

The screen splutters with white noise for a few moments, trying to acquire the feed from the phone camera.

But the image steadies and footage of the office ceiling appears on the screen, pulled out of the phone's camera by Fuchs's spyware. The phone itself is quiet and dark, giving no indication that it's doing anything at all.

Seeing the spyware in action once again gives me the chills. Who is Fuchs spying on right now? Someone I know?

"Son of a bitch," I mutter. Fuchs's going to pay for this.

"Exactly," January says. "Now let's see if I've managed to make something that can stop him."

"You did."

She doesn't answer. Instead, she opens a new command window, the one that controls Ultra. A few lines of code to tell it to go to work, and then she hits the Enter key again.

Her shoulders are rigid with tension, so I knead some of

it out as we wait. The feed from the phone camera remains crisp and clear.

Come on, I tell her program. *Do your damn job.*

It doesn't listen.

January sighs, the sound filled with infinite sadness and defeat.

Fuck. Fuck, fuck, fuck. I can't say if I'm more disappointed for her or for missing the chance to nail Fuchs's balls to the wall.

And then the camera feed splinters. It goes clear again, briefly, and then it's nothing but white noise.

January snaps into action, calling up the window that controls the spyware program. It's still running, still trying to pull images off the camera's phone... but it can't decode what it's getting anymore. Ultra has encrypted the data.

"You did it." Elation fills me. "January, this is—"

She shakes her head. "It's encrypting fine, but I need to make sure I can decode it. Nobody wants their pictures turned into white noise permanently."

She calls up the Ultra command window and routes the encrypted images into it, telling Ultra to unscramble them.

This time the program doesn't tease us with more sputters and white noise. The second January hits Enter, the video feed is there, crisp and bright as if we were looking on the phone screen itself.

"You're amazing." I press another kiss to her hair. "Completely and totally amazing."

She sags under my hands as if she can't quite believe what's happened. "It worked. I mean, it's only the first test—"

I spin her chair around and crouch before her. "No. We can take this to Pixio right now. This is more than enough to convince them."

Her brow furrows. "Are you sure?"

"Trust me." I slip my hands into hers and hold tight. "I'll do the selling. You just bring the hardware."

For a moment the uncertainty holds on to her. She doesn't want to believe. But then everything about her goes light, as if I've taken a weight from her.

"Okay. You're in charge of the deal making then. I trust you."

I feel that in every inch of myself. This project is everything to her. She's got everything riding on this.

And she trusts me with it.

"I love you." I hadn't meant to say that, but it feels like the only right thing to say here.

Her expression freezes. She's stunned, and I can't tell if it's in a good way. My heart freezes too.

I'm vulnerable all over again with her, worse than I was in college though, because this isn't a crush.

It's love.

I can have anything in the world I want, but all I want is her to love me in return.

January swallows, slow and deliberate. "You... you love *me?*" Then she pulls her hands from mine and covers her face.

My entire body sinks. It's happening all over again. I'd thought...

She takes a shuddering breath, then another. "I never believed..." Her hands drop, and the light shining from her eyes gives me hope. "I love you too."

I never thought I could feel this much. There's nothing in my life to compare to the sensations flooding through me. I stand up, pull her out of the chair and into my arms.

"I'll give you everything you've ever wanted," I promise her. "The entire world. You just have to ask."

She laughs into my chest. "How about your heart? Can I have that?"

"It was always yours." It's true; she's been carrying it since college, and I've only just realized it. "But I'd like to make a deal. Can I have yours in return?"

January lifts her face to mine. "Done," she says, right before we seal our bargain with a kiss.

CHAPTER 24

January

I can't sleep.

After the night I've had with Mark, I should be dead to the world like he is. And I'm definitely tired, my muscles pleasantly sore from all the orgasms, but my mind is also reeling from everything that's happened.

My program works.

And Mark loves me.

I've been staring into the dark for what seems like hours, Mark's arm thrown over my waist, as I repeat those two facts over and over. They both seem unreal. And wonderful.

Mark shifts next to me, pressing his face into my shoulder, his arm tightening around me. He makes a noise of mumbled pleasure, like he's happy to have found me even in his sleep.

I gently kiss his forehead. "I'll be back," I whisper, then slip out of the bed.

He mutters darkly, his arm searching again, but then he stills. I can't help but push back his hair, so thick and dark. When he's asleep like this, his chest bare, his power isn't from his wealth or all the trappings of it—it's all him.

But I should let him sleep and take advantage of my

insomnia. No matter what Mark thinks, there're still some bugs that have to be worked out.

I settle into my chair in the office space, the château deeply quiet around me. The whir of my laptop fan is almost too loud.

I stretch and yawn, trying to find a comfortable position. I'm tempted to head back to bed, but I know I'll only stare at nothing for several hours more. And there's still work to do.

So I call up my code and pull out the list of bugs I need to deal with. It's tedious, mind-numbing work, perfect for a night when I can't sleep.

When my new phone pings, I'm more than ready for a distraction. I loaded my secure messaging app on the new phone before we left, just in case Grace contacted me. When I see the little red notification in the messenger app, my smile is so wide it hurts.

If she can message me, she must be okay. My rejection of Fuchs's offer didn't put her in jeopardy, thank God.

When I open the message, I go so cold I start to shiver. All the way down to my bones.

You should have taken the offer, Miss Harris.

He's found us both out. The only way he could send this message is if he has Grace's phone. Which means he knows she sent me the documents.

Oh fuck. My heart drums out a steadily increasing beat of panic. *What have you done to Grace?* I type.

I can feel the sneer in his reply: *Your co-conspirator is perfectly safe. I don't indulge in physical violence.*

He's said she's safe, but I'm even more frightened now. Thick in that is the implication that Grace may not be safe for long and that while he doesn't do *physical* violence, there's an entire host of other tortures he could use.

If he knows what Grace and I have done, why hasn't he told the authorities? Or at least fired her?

What do you want from me? I ask baldly. I'm too panicked to dance around the issue with him.

He doesn't answer, at least not with words. Instead, picture after picture comes through, all of them blurred, like they were captured while someone was running with their phone. But I can see a picture on a wall, a chair by a table, and a dog's tail. Enough to recognize what he's sending me.

Fuchs has activated his spyware on one of my parents' phones, sending me images of my childhood home. Reminding me that everyone I love is vulnerable to him.

I'm actively shivering now, my body trying to shake off all this fear. This is worse than if he'd remotely activated my phone, because my parents never did anything to him. Grace and I are the ones fighting him; we should be the only ones in danger.

You have my attention, I reply. For half a moment I consider waking up Mark and letting him take over. He's on my side. I can trust him. He can fight with me.

I push up from the desk chair, my laptop open on the desk. The bubble shows that Fuchs is typing now, but I don't want to see his reply. Except it comes through before I can shut the computer.

Good. If you'd like to finish this without any more fuss—or without endangering your associate's position—please meet me at Corvus tomorrow at five. And I wouldn't tell Mr. Taylor about this.

That's not all Fuchs has sent. There's a video too.

If the photos left me cold, this video leaves me sick. Vilely, wrenchingly ill.

The scene is a bedroom, filmed in gauzy, low light. There's no unsettling night vision setting here—I can see everything fairly clearly. A woman walks into the frame, looking wrenchingly young. She can't be more than twenty. Something about her is familiar... maybe it's her hairstyle.

It's hard to tell because she won't face the camera—and she's naked.

A man enters then, also naked. He's familiar too. Much too much familiar, although he hasn't faced the camera yet either. But I *know* that body, the way he carries himself through space.

My heart races as I pray that it's not true. That it's not him.

But when he turns to face the camera, the Mark I knew in college stares back at me, shattering all my hopes.

I want to stop watching, but I know this is no ordinary sex tape. The sticking point isn't that Mark has been with other women—I already knew that. No, I'm supposed to see exactly which woman he's with. That's the part that's meant to hurt me.

The woman is kissing Mark now, her hand clasping his nape. There's no sound—thank God—but her posture is loose as she leans into him. She wants him, wants to be in that moment with him. He's kissing her back but without as much enthusiasm. I think. The light is enough to identify them but not enough to read the finer details of their expressions.

Again the familiarity of the woman catches at me. I know her. I'm sure of it.

In a sickening rush, I realize who it might be. The one person who would be the worst betrayal.

No. No, Mark wouldn't have done that. Not to her, and he wouldn't have lied to me. He told me he loved me.

When the woman finally turns to the camera, a pleasure-soaked smile on her face, I already know who it is. But my heart still shatters.

Chloe's as young and innocent as Mark is. She has no idea how her life is about to blow up thanks to some pictures like these. She pulls him down to the bed, her mouth open on a laugh.

The video ends there. There's more, I'm sure, but perhaps he'll deploy the rest if I remain stubborn.

I have no idea how he got this, but it's clear he's done his research. Only someone who's dug deep into my past and Mark's would have found out about Chloe. And Fuchs must have dug deep enough to find this.

The text bubble on his end pops up—apparently he's got more to say.

If you refuse my buyout offer, this video goes to every major newspaper tomorrow, along with TidBytes. *How long before it hits over a million views, do you think?*

Under an hour, I'd guess. Mark will be instantly recognizable, which will fuel the spread of the video. And within a day or so, they'll identify Chloe too. The horrible stuff that happened to her at Stanford will be dragged out again, along with the revenge porn her ex put out on the internet. Revenge porn that Mark himself might have passed around, commented on. Mark can weather something like a sex tape perfectly fine, but this will tear Chloe's life apart. Again.

Fuchs is still there, waiting for me to respond to this. Knowing that he's dealt me a killing blow.

With shaking hands, I type out, *You've made your point. I'll be there.*

I'll be waiting. He disconnects then, having won everything he could have ever wanted.

I gather up my laptop, my messenger bag, and my phone. I leave behind everything else Mark's bought me—the electronics, the clothes, the jewelry.

And I leave him still asleep.

I'd say that I never looked back, but that would be a lie. Even after everything I've seen, I still look back.

CHAPTER 25

When I wake up, I immediately know something is wrong.

January isn't here. The bed is cold, which means she hasn't been here for a while.

She's woken up before in the middle of the night, but she's always come back to bed at some point. I've woken up with her for a week.

But she's not here now.

I walk through the house toward the office, looking for her. This feeling of mine is irrational—she has to be here. She wouldn't leave without telling me. And where would she go?

When I get to the office, adrenaline spikes through my veins.

Arranged carefully on her desk are the phone, earrings, and tennis bracelet I got her. She hasn't taken the jewelry off since I gave it to her, not even in the shower.

Her laptop is gone though. And the room feels... cold, in a way it never did before.

There's a message here, and when the full impact of it hits me, I stop breathing.

She's rejected me. Again.

My fist opens and closes, the rest of me utterly paralyzed. I'm hollowed out, empty. I gave her everything of me... and she rejected it.

I don't understand. Not why she left or how I can hurt like I've been hit by a semi. I can't even get angry at her disappearance.

There's just... nothing inside.

I somehow make my way around her desk, falling into her chair. She'd sit here, right across from me, typing away on her battered laptop. And now there's nothing left but the gifts I gave her.

The earrings are cold and hard when I pick them up, not even a hint of her body heat remaining. The stones are dull in the low light from the hallway. They would gleam brightly enough to make me blink when they were in her ears.

I love you.

She said that just tonight. And then she just... *fucking left me.*

My fist smashes into the desk. Some part of my brain flinches at the pain and noise.

That flinch becomes a crack. And then a fissure, and suddenly I realize how dumb I'm being.

When she rejected me before, January did it right to my face. Yeah, I was hurt and pissed at the time, but she didn't ghost me or anything.

And she's kept secrets from me but only to protect her friend. Which means...

I raise my head and stare into the darkness. "Fucking Fuchs. He did this."

She was frightened when she first came to me. And she's frightened now. He did something to make her bolt without a word.

The adrenaline jumping through me turns to ice. He must

have threatened her. Kidnapped her. He wants her company, and a man like Fuchs doesn't take no for an answer.

He's about to find out a man like me isn't going to let him get away with this. A man like me is going to do everything and anything to find the woman he loves, then utterly ruin the asshole who dared to take her.

I tear outside and jump into the Tesla. Before the car door fully shuts, I'm gunning it down the driveway, rocketing toward the City, praying I make it in time.

Finn is the one to catch me as I careen into Bastard Capital.

"Whoa, whoa, whoa!" Finn clotheslines me as I try to barrel past him toward my office. I'd never let the Tesla drop below a hundred as I raced back to the City and on to Sand Hill Road.

January was gone, all her things left behind. Every second counted now that Fuchs had grabbed her.

"Let go," I snarl. "He's got her, and I have to get her back. And then smash that fucker into a million pieces."

I take a breath and size up Finn. I'm not a small dude, but he's got a few inches and several pounds of muscle on me. Like, boxer-type muscle, which is good in a fight. "You're coming with me. I might need backup."

Finn's arm tightens around me, squeezing hard on my windpipe. "Dude, you need to chill the fuck out. I've got your back any day of the week, but I have no fucking clue what's going on."

Like I've got the time to explain. "Fuchs has January. I'm getting her back."

"Is he here?" Logan roars from his office. "Because Mark needs to explain some shit fast."

When he barrels into the hallway, Anjie is close on his heels, looking worried. "Mark?" she asks in a quavering voice.

Jesus. I was holding it together, but the fear in Anjie's voice cracks my shell of anger, letting my own fear seep out.

"I'll make sure she's fine," I promise Anjie. "I'll save her."

"What the hell is going on with Ultra?" Logan's put his hands on his hips. "I thought we weren't selling to Fuchs."

"What?"

"It's in *TidBytes* today," Finn explains, relaxing his grip on me. "A big story about how Ultra is being sold to Corvus." He drops his voice. "Along with some pictures of Callie with Julian."

That explains Logan's mood, but I don't have time to deal with it. Logan knows the woman he loves is safe, if not in his arms. Whereas January could be anywhere. Fuchs might have done anything to her.

"Why the hell would *TidBytes* have the announcement?" I ask. "It's only a gossip blog."

Anjie shrugs. "We were hoping you could explain."

"We had her system working. It was a great test, and I told her we were ready to take it to Pixio... and..."

Logan's expression falls. "Oh shit. What happened?"

"She was just gone the next morning. Didn't take anything except her laptop and her phone. I've called her phone, her house, her office, even her parents—nobody knows where she is. Somehow Fuchs must have gotten to her. Or kidnapped her. That's why the sale announcement is already out."

Finn pushes me toward the conference room. "Anjie, can you make some coffee and call in everyone else? We've got some planning to do."

By the time everyone assembles in the conference room, Anjie included, I'm worked up to a fever pitch again, pacing like a caged wolf.

"We're wasting too much time," I say, punching my fist

into my palm. "He's got her, and we have to rescue her. There's no other explanation."

Dev raises an eyebrow. "Really? How are you going to rescue her?"

"Storm Corvus's offices."

Elliot's head snaps up. "That's illegal."

"I don't give a shit! I know that fucker has her, and I'm getting her back!"

Dev, that asshole, remains cool as I rant, which only pisses me off more. "So you're going to charge into Fuchs's secure building," he says, "somehow find his office before security tackles you, and demand that he release January?"

"Fucking yes, you cold-blooded bastard!"

"Assuming he has taken her—which you don't know, maybe she left for some other reason—why would he hold her in his office building? He knows that's the first place we'll look. Or the authorities will."

He's making sense, which only infuriates me more. "Well, what do you suggest?"

"Was anything wrong before she left?"

I take a sharp, jerking breath as I remember. *I love you.* I'll die remembering exactly how January said that. "God, no."

"Think."

I try to, but all that comes is memories of her softness, of how close we'd been. How much I loved her and maybe always had.

"There's nothing," I say. "But Fuchs can spy on anyone anywhere. Maybe… maybe he found something incriminating. Threatened her with it."

"But we never found anything in the background check," Anjie says. "Why wouldn't she tell you if Fuchs had threatened her? Why disappear?"

"Fuchs found out about her friend sending her those documents." But even as I say it, it doesn't make sense.

January would have told me about that. "It's the only thing he could have on her."

Because maybe Fuchs didn't threaten her. Maybe he threatened someone close to her. But that still makes no sense. If the threat was to Grace or...

It suddenly dawns on me. "He threatened *me*."

"Pardon?" Dev says.

"Me." I tap my chest. "Fuchs must have threatened me with... something. So January took off to protect me."

It's a beautiful gesture that's equal parts touching and infuriating. I protect her, not the other way around. I'll have to make that very clear once I find her.

"What could that be?" Finn asks.

I shrug. "Hell if I know. Whatever it is, it can't be that bad. The question now is, has January signed the contracts? And how do we stop her from doing that?"

Elliot looks thoughtful. "If she hasn't signed yet, that makes it easy. But even if she has, a contract signed under duress isn't legal. Both parties have to understand what they're agreeing to. One could argue that January was under such extreme emotional stress she wouldn't be competent to understand what she'd signed."

"You mean, you could argue it. And win."

Elliot chews on that. "Fuchs is going to have some damn good lawyers, but so will we. Then there's the luck of the draw with judges, but he might not want to risk the exposure of a lawsuit. His company needs the shadows to operate. And his government clients won't like it either."

"Do you think he won't prosecute the documents leak then?" I ask. Not only could he fire Grace and invalidate her visa, he could have her sent to jail for corporate espionage. Maybe even January too.

Elliot's fingers drum on the table. "We can't completely rule it out, but my guess would be he'd want to keep that quiet too. It looks bad to his clients, and he can continue to use it as leverage against January if he keeps it quiet."

A plan begins to form in my mind. There's a ton of moving parts, things that need to mesh perfectly in order for it to work... but I can see a way out. And a way to defeat Fuchs.

"We need to schedule a meeting with Pixio. Tomorrow."

Anjie nods and pulls out her phone. Thank God for her.

"Without January?" Logan asks.

"Oh no, we're definitely getting her out. We need to hit Fuchs back though." At Elliot's look, I say, "Not physically. Whatever Fuchs has on January—we need something worse on him."

Elliot looks like he's about to protest, but Paul cuts in. "Mark's right. If we stop Fuchs from buying Ultra, he'll be pissed. He'll feel we stole it from him. And he'll want to strike back."

"We need a shield then. Do any of you know anything about him? Anything personal?" Even though we move in the same circles, I hardly know anything about Fuchs. He's not married, has no kids, doesn't date. I'm beginning to suspect no one knows much about him beyond rumors.

"Blackmail?" Logan sounds skeptical.

"Yeah, blackmail," I say. Logan doesn't need to be a Goody Two-shoes about this. "This fucker wants to record everyone in America. Let's turn the tables on him."

"Okay, like what?" Finn asks.

"I don't know him." Paul lifts his palms. "Nobody I know does either."

Elliot makes a face when we all turn to him. "How am I supposed to know him? All I know is that his assistant is annoying."

Logan just shakes his head.

"Fuck," I mutter. So much for some good old-fashioned

social engineering to help us here. We could hack Fuchs's phone and computer, but we don't have time for that. So we're shit out of luck. Except—

"Dev?" As I turn to him, I realize he's been quiet. Way too quiet. "What do you know about him?"

Dev is doing his usual man-of-mystery bullshit, but I don't have time for it. He folds his hands and exhales. "I've heard rumors," Dev finally says. "That he's into... rougher stuff. Dark stuff."

"Like what, BDSM?" I almost laugh. "That's practically vanilla these days. He's not going to care who knows that."

Dev raises a finger. "But remember who we're dealing with. It's not how the public would react to the news—it's how he would react to it being public."

"He'd freak out."

Dev nods. "Also, he's not the one holding the whip."

I release a long breath as I sit back. I really don't give a shit what Fuchs gets up to in his spare time—if a session with a bullwhip on his ass helps him unwind, good for him—but if I can use this against him, I will.

"Do you have any real proof?" I ask. Fuchs will only laugh off rumors. Or maybe not—but I still want something concrete in my hands when I confront him.

Dev shakes his head. "Only whispers."

"Shit." I pop my jaw back and forth. "I'll just have to bull-shit my way through then."

"You're really good at bullshit," Finn offers. He turns to Dev. "How the hell did you hear that about Fuchs?"

"I listen," is all Dev will say.

Anjie sets her phone down, her expression sober. "Jack, the CEO of Pixio, is going to be in a meeting all day tomorrow, then he's flying out to Aspen for two weeks. The best I could get you is half an hour at lunch tomorrow."

"I'll take it. Trust me, January's demo will only need ten

minutes to blow him away." A wicked thought occurs to me, one way to really twist the knife in Fuchs. "Tell him we'll meet at Roasted for lunch. Exactly at twelve thirty."

Anjie raises her brows, but she goes off to call Jack's assistant back. It's an odd request, but I'm confident Anjie will make it work.

All the pieces are coming together except for the very last one. The most important one.

"I hate to point out any flaws in your plan," Paul says, "but you've just scheduled a meeting without having found January. You don't even know if she's signed the paperwork with Corvus yet. And if she's not answering her phone..."

"I've got a plan for that too." I get up from the chair and gesture to Finn. "The rest of you keep looking for dirt on Fuchs. Call me if you find anything. Finn, you and I are going to pay a visit to Ultra."

I just hope the team January put together is as good as it needs to be.

CHAPTER 26

 January

My apartment door won't unlock. And because I'm an utter mess, I start sobbing, right there on the stoop.

I know this door is tricky, that I need to be patient and put the key in just so and maybe jiggle it as I turn it, but instead I want to smash my fists into the door until it gives. Which would be awesome, because our landlord would definitely charge us to fix that.

There's also the issue of my Lyft driver watching from her car window, probably wondering why I've come all the way from Napa and why I'm about to collapse outside my apartment door.

I give her a tight smile and a wave. "Go away," I mutter.

I pull the key out, then wrench it forward, putting most of my weight behind it. It probably won't help unlock the damn thing, but it feels better than nothing. I put my shoulder to the door and shove as I twist the key.

My shoulder is starting to ache when my roommate John opens the door. I catch myself before I can smash into him.

"January!" He's got a bowl of cereal in his hands. "Haven't seen you in forever. You look like hell. What's up?"

"Been working," I say as I rub my eyes. I'm way too close to crying.

He steps aside to let me in. "Congrats on the sale—I saw the news in *TidBytes*."

I stop dead in front of the coatrack. "What?"

My tone makes his eyes go wide. "The, uh, sale. Of Ultra to Corvus." He swallows hard. "I mean, it's all over the tech news."

Oh shit. I haven't even spoken to Fuchs or signed anything, and he's already announcing it as done. And there's nothing I can do about it.

"Right," I say slowly, trying to think of some suitable lie. "It's just, it's not entirely final yet. I was surprised is all."

He gestures with the bowl. "Well, congratulations. I bet you'll be even more surprised once all those millions end up in your bank account."

"You have no idea." I pull my phone out of my bag. I wanted to be well away from Napa—and Mark—before I turned it back on.

About a dozen text messages from Doc instantly shout at me along with a notification of ten voice mails. So I see she's already heard the news. I feel like the worst person in the world, letting her hang out to dry like this, but I can't tell her anything, not until it's all over.

I'm so, so sorry, Doc. I hope we can still be friends after this.

There are also many, many texts and voice mails from Mark. I delete each and every one with shaking hands, taking care not to actually read the messages.

"Um." John clears his throat, and I look up from my phone. Shoot, he's still here. "There's been a bunch of people calling me, asking where you are. Is everything okay?"

I hold up my phone. "I shut this off so I could think, you know? And people freak out these days when you don't text them back in half a second."

I don't know if John buys that since his nod is stiff, uncertain. But he lets it go. "Could we maybe talk about all the stuff that was delivered then?"

"What stuff—" My mouth drops open as I finally take notice, real notice, of our living room and kitchen—in our apartment, they're basically the same room. And it's filled with stuff we never had before. A new couch, a fancy coffee machine, a juicer that costs more than our rent... and I have a feeling there's more that I'm not seeing.

"Holy hell," I breathe.

"Yeah," John says, setting his bowl on the counter. "It showed up Tuesday. And the person in charge said we've got a laundry service now, we just have to leave the bag out on Fridays."

"Who brought this?" Although I think I already know the answer. "Let me guess, has a lot of tattoos, dresses like a pinup girl?"

John brightens. "That's her. Is she, uh, working for you?"

"No," I say as I continue to take in all this new stuff. "And she's... *involved* with someone."

Maybe involved is overstating it, but there's definitely something between her and Dev. Oh, and I'm also about to betray everyone at Bastard Capital when I sell Ultra.

And Mark...

My throat closes. Mark did all this for me, arranging it while were together in Napa. Even when I was with him, he couldn't stop secretly taking care of me.

Did he take care of Chloe, back when they were sleeping together? And did he turn on her when everyone else did?

Will he turn on me as brutally when he finds me gone or when he reads the front page of *TidBytes*?

I ache at the very thought, which is so, so perverse of me, given that I've seen that video. But my heart is lagging behind my head—it's not ready to give up on Mark and what we might have.

I press a finger to my temple, trying to push out the pain. "Could you do me a favor?" I ask John in a voice too thick for my throat. "If anybody comes by to see me or calls, can you tell them I'm not here?"

I have eight hours until I have to meet my fate in the form of Arne Fuchs. I'm going to take that time to curl up on my bed, pull the covers over my head, and wish my life was anything but this.

"Are you sure everything is okay? You look awful."

John's right to be confused—I should be over the moon with the news about Corvus. But while he is my roommate, we're not exactly close. He never asked about Grace once she moved out, and I don't think he'd miss me much if I left either. He's not a bad roommate, but he's not a true friend either.

I summon a weak smile. It hurts my cheeks. "With everything going on, I've got a killer headache." I gesture toward my room. "I'm going to sleep it off before I head back out tonight."

"Sure." John smiles with relief. Of course he wants an easy explanation here. "Congratulations again."

I give a wave over my shoulder as I head to my room. When the door shuts behind me, I let myself collapse on the bed. It smells musty after a week of my not being here. Nothing like the sheets on the bed Mark and I shared in Napa. Or the bed in his house.

I pull the blanket around me and tuck my knees up into my chest, enclosing myself in a cave of dark warmth.

CHAPTER 27

When I slam the Tesla to a screeching halt in front of the secure building where we've stashed Ultra, Finn pops the door open before the car's even come to a complete stop.

"Jesus," he snaps as he hops out to stable ground. I don't think I've ever seen him look so white. "I think I left my lunch back in Los Altos."

"Don't be such a baby." I slam the car door shut. "You've driven sand rails off cliffs before."

"Yeah, and that was a nicer ride than the one you just gave me."

I ignore him—are we in a race against time or not?—and burst into the offices.

They look up in surprise, all of them gathered around Doc's desk. Dark circles and tight brows mark them, the signs of long nights filled with too much coffee and anxiety. Well, they'd better get ready for a few more all-nighters.

"We are not selling to Corvus." Doc announces that with a jut of her chin. She bursts out of her chair, ready for battle. "I don't care what you told January, but we get a say too. And none of us want to work for that asshole."

They form up behind the desk as if it's a barricade, ready to defend Ultra.

Yep, January really did pick the right team here.

"We're not selling to Corvus," I say. "I swear."

"Then why's it in all the news sites?" Doc gestures with a fist to her laptop. "January never told us, and she's not answering her phone or her emails. What did you do to her?"

"I love her." I can't think of any better way to say how I feel about January. Love covers pretty much everything in me that's hers.

Several of the coders go "awww," their posture loosening. Doc isn't having it though.

"We love January too. Now, what have you done with her, asshole?"

In under a minute, I sketch out everything for the team, starting with Grace handing over the Corvus plans to January and ending with the Bastards' meeting half an hour ago. They're all smart women, and they figure things out about twenty seconds into my spiel.

"Okay." Doc goes to a whiteboard and begins to erase it. "So we've got to get Ultra polished enough to demo it for Pixio tomorrow."

I nod. "That's the easy part, right?"

"Yep." Doc points out three women. "You guys are on that." She writes Demo on the board and underlines it. "We've got that handled," she says to me. "But what about January? Has she signed the contracts already?" She looks Finn up and down. "And what are you doing here?"

Even though this is all deadly serious, I have to bite my cheek to keep from laughing at Finn's expression.

"I'm Finn," he rumbles through his beard.

"Can you code?"

He blinks at her. "Can I— Are you for real?"

Doc shoos him toward the women working on the demo. "Go help them then. And try not to screw anything up."

Finn gives me a look that says *How the hell does she not know who I am?*

I shrug. "You heard the lady."

Finn sighs, then cracks his knuckles as he heads over to a terminal. He might be putting on a show of reluctance, but he'll be happier than a pig in shit to get inside Ultra's code.

Doc taps her marker against the whiteboard. "What about January?"

"She won't answer my calls or my texts either," I say. "I don't know why. But she's got to be communicating with Fuchs somehow."

A light comes into Doc's eyes, and I can tell she's already skipping ahead of me. "It won't be easy."

"I know." My smile is wry. "She's probably running Ultra on her own phone."

Doc's smile is wider than mine. "Thank God I helped design it then. Can you help with that? It's going to be a bitch to crack, even with my inside information."

I nod. "Anything I can do to help."

Doc gestures me to a workstation. "You can use that machine."

"So, what are we doing?" one of the women still standing around asks.

Doc pulls a chair up next to me. "We're hacking January's phone. We've got to find everything she might have sent to Fuchs and figure out if and where she's going to meet him." She flicks her hand at them. "Get to it. We don't know how much time we have, and this is going to take all of us working on it."

Within five seconds, everyone in the room is madly typing away at a terminal, coding like fiends.

We're coming for you, I promise January.

CHAPTER 28

January

The Corvus building is a tower of steel and glass, just like every other office building ever built in the past thirty years. But somehow this particular arrangement of gleaming metal and flashing glass puts me in mind of a coffin.

Maybe it's because I'm coming here to bury my company.

I technically have fifteen minutes before I'm supposed to meet Fuchs, but I don't wait to go in. I want this over as soon as possible. There's no point drawing out the suffering.

My heels click on the pavement, snip snip snip, and I've dressed to impress. Not the clothes Mark gave me but something he's never seen me in before—gray tweed pencil skirt with a kick pleat, a sea-green silk tank that clings to me, and a black woolen jacket in an Edwardian cut. And my shoes are high-heeled patent leather Mary Janes, sexy and severe all at once. I look amazing.

I feel terrible. But at least my outfit will detract from my ashen expression.

There's nothing in the entryway of the Corvus offices except two steel doors and a security desk. There isn't even a sign announcing what this place is. The guards are wearing black suits with skinny ties and earpieces, like they're Secret Service or something.

"Miss?" one says as I approach. There's a warning there: if you stumbled in here on accident, stumble right back out.

"I have a meeting with Fuchs." I don't let him rattle me—he's not my opponent.

He types away at a terminal, which is set into the desk so that I can't see it. After several long moments, there's the whirring of a printer and then he hands over a badge, still warm from being printed. It's got my name and my photo on it, taken when I walked into the building.

Jesus, this place is already crazy, and I haven't even walked inside.

"This is coded to allow you into the conference room on the first floor," he explains. "And only that room."

"And if I need to use the restroom?"

His eyebrows shoot up. "Hold it."

The steel doors swing open then with a thick, metallic clatter, like a bank vault opening.

"Thanks," I say as I walk in. He doesn't answer.

There are no numbers on the doors, no directory in the hallway. Just an endless corridor of closed doors. The massive doors behind me slip shut, and I can feel the HVAC repressurizing, blowing my hair up as it seals us from the outside air.

I start to shiver although I'm fighting the chills as hard as I can. The temperature must be close to sixty, and with the HVAC blowing, it feels even colder.

This place is awful and unwelcoming, and when Fuchs buys my company, I'll have to work here. That's how it works—big company buys a small company, and everyone at the small company gets cushy jobs and great stock options at big company.

That will have to be something I negotiate for my team—

buyout offers without employment offers. They'll thank me for it, I'm sure. That'll be the only thing they'll be thanking me for in all this.

I resettle my messenger bag on my shoulder and look right and left down the hall, wondering if I should start trying doors. I finally catch sight of a small, unobtrusive sign to the left: CONFERENCE ROOM. An arrow points me down that hall.

When I come to the only door that's labeled—the sign announces I've found the conference room—the latch snicks open as soon as I approach.

I want to wait, to catch my breath, to give one small whimper, but if I hesitate too long, the door will lock again. I have to move forward.

The room is as sterile as the rest of this building, cold and bare except for a long table and some chairs. In the middle of the table is a bowl of too-perfect apples, red and shiny and completely unappealing.

Coldest of all is Fuchs's expression as he waits at the head of the table. Next to him is his horrible assistant, Minerva Dyne, wearing a hint of a smile.

I'm frightened of Fuchs, but I'm enraged at her. How dare she smile when I'm about to sell away all my dreams?

So I focus on him, the better to get ahold of myself. He looks... completely normal. I've passed thousands of men who look exactly like him on the streets of San Francisco every day, all of them stamped with the generic programmer look.

He stares back without saying a word. I wonder if I'm anything like what he was expecting. Or maybe he didn't even form a mental image of me—I might not have even gotten that much consideration from him.

I set my bag on one of the chairs, but I don't sit down. My

legs insist that I need to be ready to fly at a moment's notice. Only, where would I go?

Fuchs pushes a set of papers toward me with those little colored signature tags stuck everywhere inside. They're so bright and cheery, so out of place in this austere room I do a double take.

"Sign and everything will be taken care of."

I jump, because I've never heard his voice before. It's as ordinary as his appearance, although I might be hearing a hint of an accent. Or maybe I'm searching too hard for something sinister about him.

"What about Grace?"

There's a flicker in Minerva's expression. There's nothing in Fuchs's.

"Her employment won't be terminated," he says, "if you sign."

"And my team? They want severance packages, not employment offers."

Minerva sneers. "We don't want them. Just you. And the encryption program." When I don't move, she goes on, "Their offers are more than generous. They'll never have to work again."

"And they have their own noncompetes," Fuchs says. "They can never work in cryptology again."

I take a sharp breath, but my lungs refuse to fill. I can't do this, can't sign and decide their futures for them. They'll hate me forever.

But there's Grace and Chloe on the other side, and if don't sign, they'll suffer. Perhaps worse than my team would.

"And me?" I don't even care what happens to me, but some instinct, some last flutter of curiosity, has me asking.

"You'll work here. On perfecting Ultra."

"To what end?"

"That's for Corvus to decide."

Meaning that I'll work on something that will never see the light of day.

I stare at the contract. No matter what it says, I don't have much leverage here. Not compared to what he's holding. Still, I can't bring myself to pick up the pen and end this.

"My lawyer…" I gesture at the contract even though I'm stalling at this point.

"Wouldn't change a thing in this," Minerva says, smooth and cold as glass.

"Should I remind you of why you're signing?" Fuchs asks. "Or give you more reasons to do so?"

What, like more of the horrid video? Or some evidence that he's currently spying on Chloe, ready to have all this blow right back at her when the video becomes public?

I grab the pen. "You were quite convincing in our first conversation."

Signing a contract like this is different from signing a credit card slip. A lazy, thoughtless scrawl won't work. No, you have to sign deliberately so they know it's your signature and you mean it. I flip to the first sticky note where a line waits for my name. Waits for me to make this all official and ruin everything.

Too bad I have to ruin everything to save Chloe and Grace.

I start on *January*, making the loops of the *J* and the *Y* just so rather than losing them in the curves of the other letters. I pause for half a moment, inspect what I've done. It certainly looks official. The pen nib sinks back down, ready to start on the *H*. Ready to end it all.

Just as I pull the pen into inking the first support of the *H*, the door bursts open.

Several things happen at once. Fuchs squeals with rage and surprise, Minerva drops her mask and looks truly afraid, and I toss the pen as far away from me as I can. It rolls down the length of the conference table, coming to a rest in front of Mark.

"January." If he can see anything in the room besides me, I can't tell. His gaze is open, hungry, and hopeful, and it's devouring me. "Whatever he's told you, don't believe it. Don't sign. Whatever it is, we can fix it, together. You don't need to do this."

Don't believe what? My own eyes?

Before I can answer, the rest of the Bastards come pouring in, followed by my team at Ultra. Doc, not giving a shit that we're all in a very tense moment here, rushes over to hug me tight.

"You should have told me," she whispers in my ear.

"I couldn't," I say miserably.

She squeezes me again. "We'll talk. After."

She then heads back to rejoin this Justice League Mark has assembled. Seeing the wall of them, resolute and steely eyed, makes my throat close. They've come here to save me, only this is the absolute worst thing they could have done. Fuchs isn't going to react well to this.

"How did you get in?" he's demanding, his face a study in frigid rage. "I'm calling security."

"Don't bother. They already know we're here." Mark takes a step toward me, intending to bring me close.

I step back and shake my head. The look on his face when I do... I have to turn away so I can keep breathing.

He might be the master deal maker, but he has no idea of the dynamite Fuchs is holding. One wrong move and we all go up in smoke.

Fuchs has brought his rage back under control and is cold once more. "This is Miss Harris's decision. You have no part in it." He turns to me. "Tell them."

It takes a massive effort to get the words out. "This is my choice. It's for the best."

"What?" Mark roars like a lion. "After what he's done? What did he do to you? How could you do this?" His expression turns pleading. "Whatever it is, January, I don't care. Whatever he has on you or on me—it doesn't matter."

He couldn't have chosen a better weapon to cut my heart out. I have to wrap my arms around myself to keep all my feelings from spilling out.

"Are you accusing me of blackmail?" Fuchs is practically daring Mark to say it.

Mark, of course, takes the bait. "You're damn right. And I've got some blackmail of my own."

Oh no. My skin goes cold and I can't catch my breath. What the hell is Mark talking about?

If Mark pulls the trigger on his blackmail, Fuchs will retaliate. And Chloe's life will be ruined all over again.

"Wait." I hold out my hands between them as if I might actually stop them. "Mark, please don't do this."

There's a gasp from everyone else, but Mark is silent, and his face... I think I've broken his heart.

I press on. "I know what I'm doing. It's still my company. I can do what I want."

I can read his face by now, as clearly as I can lines of code. He thought we were in this together, that I'd do the programming and he'd do the deal, and together we'd stop Fuchs.

But that was when I thought he was a prince among men, above all the horrible things lesser men do.

He's not. He used Chloe as surely as the rest of them did. I'm all alone again, even with over a dozen people in this conference room who've come to save me.

"I'll sign," I say to Fuchs.

But before I can grab the pen again, Mark is talking. "If you don't let her go, we'll tell everyone about your housekeeper. And leak the video we have."

Oh God, no. I put a hand to my chest as my heart threatens to burst out of my rib cage. Fuchs is going to release his own video then, and Chloe will be hurt all over again. And Grace... Who knows what Fuchs will do to her now?

Mark looks triumphant, thinking he's won, that he's outdealt Fuchs. And Fuchs...

The rage on his face is something to behold. I'm terrified, and he hasn't even moved a muscle. Whatever is going on with the housekeeper, it's clearly not something he wanted anyone to ever know.

"I've changed my mind." Fuchs bites that off and spits it out. "I don't want to buy your company—you don't deserve my money. Instead, I'm going to bury your company and leave you penniless."

Everyone starts shouting, me in protest and everyone else in victory. Minerva is the only quiet one. She looks like she's filing something away—maybe the tidbit about the housekeeper.

Fuchs takes no notice of any of it. He presses a button under the table and a voice says, "Yes?" from the ceiling.

"Tell Grace that she's terminated. Escort her to the lobby and see to it that her belongings are packed and sent on to her. Do not under any circumstances allow her to access her desk or her quarters."

"Wait." I lift my palm, not looking at my team or the Bastards. "We can still make a deal. Grace doesn't need to be punished."

"Yes, she does." Fuchs's gaze rakes everyone. "You all do and you all will be."

Hell. Desperation jumps into my throat. "I'll leak those documents."

It's the only threat I have left, a tiny stone compared to what Fuchs will throw at me.

"And I'll send Grace to jail," he says, completely unmoved. "For a very long time."

My shoulders slump. At least he's not going to press charges. One minuscule win in all this mess. Except he said we had to be *punished.* "And the video?"

Fuchs doesn't answer me. Instead, he goes for the door, Minerva tripping at his heels. Without a word, he leaves.

I get the message though. He's going to bury my company, kick my friend out of the country, and maybe, just maybe, release that video and ruin even more lives.

There's dead silence in the conference room. I can tell they're all waiting for an explanation, for me to give them some meaning here.

But I can't. Not right now. I can only do one thing, the thing I set out to do from the very beginning: go get Grace and take her from here.

CHAPTER 29

January

I can't look at Mark.

He's driving us to the hotel where we'll put Grace for the night. Grace and I are in the back seat, talking quietly together. I can still hardly believe she's here and that things went so terribly wrong. Which I've said multiple times, but I say it again now.

"I'm so sorry. I never meant for this to happen." I squeeze my fingers hard together as my stomach turns. The guilt is so thick in me it's coating my tongue, sour as rotten milk.

Grace shakes her head wearily. "I knew something like this would have to happen. I couldn't stay there and keep working on that horrible program."

"We'll figure out a way for you to stay. Mark—the Bastards know some excellent immigration lawyers."

"That's right." Mark's gaze is hard on us, watching through the rearview mirror, so tight I can feel it even though I refuse to look up. "Don't worry at all about that right now."

"Even if I can stay, I'll never find work again. Not once Fuchs is done trashing my name."

I reach out for Grace's hand. "You can work for me. At Ultra."

"That's right—you started an encryption company." She shakes her head with the hint of a smile. "I can hardly believe it."

"It's true," Mark says, the edges of his voice ragged with strain. "We've got a working prototype, and we'll be presenting to the CEO of Pixio tomorrow."

"What?" My gaze snaps to his in the mirror. "When was that arranged?"

"When you disappeared." He says it smoothly enough, but it bites anyway. "I figured that Fuchs had threatened you with something, so I thought it best to move quickly on the Ultra sale to Pixio."

My face floods with heat as I drop my head, studying my lap.

"So what was it?" It's more of a demand than a request. Mark, the master of the universe, is back.

The images from the video flood my mind, stiffen my joints. I can't talk about that, not with Grace here.

"Later," I mumble.

"Fine. We'll discuss it at the office. Along with the plan for tomorrow. You know that everyone's working their ass off for this?"

Shit, he's pissed at me. He has the right, because I did disappear and almost sell my company, but... he also doesn't, because *he fucked Chloe,* made a video of it, possibly ruined her life in college and might do it again.

"I didn't arrange this meeting." I make my voice and gaze cold, because I'm getting pissed too.

"What the fuck is going—"

"I want to help." Grace cuts across Mark's anger. "With the demonstration for tomorrow."

I blink at her. "No, you should get some rest. You've

had..." I stop, because I don't need to tell her how shitty her day has been. "We can handle it."

"I want to. Fuchs is trying to ruin my life—I want to help you stop him." She shrugs. "Otherwise I'll just spend all night watching *Futurama.*"

I smile through my pain, because Grace is such a lovely person and I've ruined everything for her, and she still wants to help. "Great." I swallow down some tears. "Doc could always use another debugger."

"Doc?"

Oh yeah, Grace has no idea who anyone is. I spend the rest of the ride filling her in so that by the time we pull up to the Bastards' secure building, she's up to speed enough to bound out of the car and say, "I'll go find Doc and get started."

Leaving Mark and me alone. Together.

"You're not going to tell me, are you? After everything we've shared"—his voice stumbles—"you're going to cut me out. Again."

I want to. I want to tell him it will never work, that we tried and too bad, that I had the right idea in college when I rejected him...

No. That's a lie. That's the easy route, which the cowardly part of my heart wants to take, not all of me.

The rest of me wants to do the dangerous thing and finally, finally, trust him even though everything is telling me I shouldn't.

"There was a video," I say quietly.

"Of us? Fuck that asshole, I'm going to bury him in lawsuits—"

"Not us."

He releases a heavy breath. "January, I don't care who you were with before."

"That's very big of you… but it wasn't me." I shiver, cold even in the heated car.

The color has left his face. "Who was I with?"

"Can you maybe guess?"

"No, I can't. You're acting like I've committed a crime, like I should already know my sentence."

God, how can he keep playing dumb like this? How many sex videos has he made? "It was *Chloe*."

Confusion stutters across his face. "Chloe? I don't even know a—" Heat rushes back into his skin, twisting his expression. "Fuck. Fuck, fuck, fuck."

"So you did make a video with her? Did you show it to all your friends, post it on the internet with all those horrible pictures, hound her out of school?" The words spill out of me along with my disgust.

"Hang on." He grabs his phone.

My mouth drops open. "What the hell do you think you're doing?"

He holds up a finger and dials a number.

I'm so appalled I simply stare. I tell him about this and he's *calling* someone?

The phone rings through the car sound system. On the third trill, a woman picks up. "Hello?"

"Chloe." Mark's mouth twitches in the ghost of a smile. "Sorry to call so late, but I've got some news."

I hold in my gasp. He's called *her*?

"No worries," she says. "Do you have a job for me?"

"Not this time. You should be sitting down."

There's a long pause. I wonder if I should announce myself, but I keep quiet. I want to hear what happens when it's only the two of them even if I'm doing the exact thing Fuchs is guilty of.

"Okay," she says slowly. "Hit me."

"Apparently someone has faked a video of you and me. A sex tape."

She gasps. "But... we've never had sex. Or even kissed!"

"I know. Like I said, it was faked. To get at me, not you," he says quickly. "This has nothing to do with what happened in college, and I swear to you, it'll never see the light of day. I will throw every last dollar I have and then some at keeping this quiet. And eventually destroying it."

Chloe's voice is wobbly, but I hear a smile in there. "I know you will. You were the only one who helped me after... Well, I don't have to tell you. I know you'll help me now."

The video plays over and over in my memories, suddenly changed. Maybe... maybe Mark's head was on at an odd angle. Maybe Chloe's skin was too smooth, her movements not quite human.

Maybe I've been had by an evil, evil man.

Mark is finishing up the call, saying goodbye to Chloe and telling her not to worry. That he'll handle everything.

I'm numb. My brain feels like it's been put on ice.

"He faked a video?" I say, mostly to myself.

Mark answers anyway. "It looks like it. How long was it?"

"He only showed me a few seconds. I thought he might be holding the rest back." Or else that was all that he had. Or faked. I run my fingers through my hair, wishing I could disappear.

"Or that was all he bothered to have made," Mark says. His voice is too steady, like he's holding it hard in place. "Faking a few seconds is much easier than an entire video."

"But... that's not easy to do."

"How much computing power do you think he has at hand?"

"God, I feel so stupid." I run a hand over my face. My skin is dry and hot, as if I've been traveling through the desert.

214

"How could I have fallen for that? I almost sold my company."

And now Fuchs has sworn to destroy me and leave me with nothing. Although I might have done all that on my own by believing that video.

Something Mark said to Chloe floats to the top of my thoughts. "She said you helped her?"

He won't look at me. "I always felt guilty because I couldn't help her in college. I didn't spread the rumors or look at the pictures, but I also couldn't stop them. So when I had the opportunity, I offered her some freelance work for Bastard Capital."

He never mentioned any of that when we were discussing Chloe before. So much could have been avoided if he'd just said something.

"You could have told me."

"You could have told *me*. I wasn't going to violate Chloe's privacy after what happened to her, not to rehash some college shit with you."

"But you just let me listen. You didn't tell her I was here."

He stares at his hands on the steering wheel for a long moment. "I suppose now after having lost you once—no, twice now—there's nothing I wouldn't do to bring you back. Even if it is at Chloe's expense."

Oh God. His voice has finally splintered, going quiet as he forces himself to finish. I can't... This hurts so damn much. For both of us.

I climb over the console, twisting myself to get close to him in the confines of the car. But I can't—this isn't the place to get close.

So I ask, "Can we finish this inside?"

CHAPTER 30

The office I've set aside for her in our secure building is as comfortable as I could manage on short notice. Or what Anjie could manage.

I nod to the Bastards assembled in the main workspace, coding away with the Ultra team in order to be ready for tomorrow. Logan catches my eye, then looks significantly at January.

I give a tiny shake of my head. I'll discuss what happened with all of them later. First, January and I need to finish this.

When I shut her office door, she doesn't sit down. Instead, she remains standing, clenching her hands together as she takes in her office.

"Is all this for me?"

There's a couch against one wall, with several pillows and a blanket, a desk with a brand-new Mac computer on it, and a few of my cousin's paintings on the walls—irises done in long strokes of purple and yellow and green, stark against a plain white background.

All this is January's. I'll give her more if she'll let me.

"This is your office, yes. Why don't you sit down?" I want

to hold her, to find comfort with her, but she won't stop pacing.

She shakes her head. "I need to move. How did you find me?"

"Doc hacked your phone. They were all worried about you."

She picks up a fountain pen from the desk, sleek and black in her long white fingers. "I never meant to hurt them. I didn't know what else to do."

"You're not alone in this. Not anymore. I'm here for you, and I always will be." I swallow hard and ask her for the one thing she's never given me, not even after she gave me her heart. "Please, trust me."

She goes still as a startled deer, and the eyes she raises to mine... wide and beautiful and brimming with tears. "I... that's what I wanted for so long. Even before I wanted you to love me."

I gather her up tightly because I'm never letting her go again. No matter what. "You can trust me. If you want to sell Ultra to Fuchs, we will. If you want me to grind that bastard into nothingness, I will. I swear, I'm at your command."

Her smile is watery. "I can tell which you'd rather do."

"It's not what I want. It's what you want. What you trust me to do."

"And if the others disagree?"

"You come first. They're a close second, but you're number one with a bullet point."

Even when she was accusing me of having hurt Chloe, I still loved her so much. Which probably proves I've fallen for her for all time.

She takes a deep breath. I can see her mind working, analyzing and weighing the options. I stay quiet, because she's the one leading me this time.

"First, I want to absolutely kill it at this meeting with Pixio."

"You will."

"Second, I want to make sure Grace can stay here."

That's going to be trickier. "Elliot's finding a lawyer as we speak."

"Third, I want to bury Fuchs and Corvus. Like, deeper than the mantle of the earth deep."

I don't remember exactly which layer of the earth that is, but I'm sure it's pretty far down. As deep as I want to bury the son of a bitch myself. "Good, because we all want to do that."

She stops, thinks some more. Then reaches up to run her fingers down the column of my neck. Shudders run through me.

"Actually, first I want to do something else." She begins to unbutton my shirt.

"Oh?" My blood is already magma hot, my cock iron hard.

"I missed you." Her fingers find my pants button.

"Jesus." I kiss every part of her bared skin I can reach, tugging at the neckline of her blouse until I hear it tear. "You have no idea how insane I went. Even Finn thought I was going overboard."

She hooks a knee around my hip, dragging us both toward the desk.

I resist. "Sweetheart, you deserve something softer."

She pushes herself up onto the desktop. "It feels like a featherbed. You make it feel like the softest surface ever."

I growl and grab her hip. "You're the soft one."

She nips at my bottom lip. "I love how hard you are. That you can be tough as steel out there but make me feel so soft when you're with me."

Our first time was on a desk, but this feels nothing like

that. As I pull her skirt up and her panties aside, this isn't some urgent, frustrated grind. It's a homecoming.

I dip my fingers into her pussy, test her wetness. So soft, so hot, ready for me. Waiting, begging.

Her arms come around my neck, holding me loosely, trusting me to stay. "I love you."

"I love you too." I reach blindly for the drawer, for the box I put in there in hopes of this exact situation. Once the condom is on, I push forward, filling her with one full thrust.

Her head falls back. "Yes, yes, this is where I need you."

I keep my movements slow but demanding, and she gives and gives and gives.

"Don't ever leave me again." I don't care that I'm begging, because I trust her with my vulnerability. I trust her with everything of me.

"I won't," she promises, her gaze holding mine. "I trust you."

I let go, my orgasm flooding me. She's clutching at me, holding on as her own climax takes her.

"I've got you," I tell her. "I'll never let you go."

Staying like this forever is something I really, really want to do, but we've got work to do. It's going to be an all-nighter, just like before finals at Stanford.

Gently I pull out of her, take care of the condom, then adjust her panties and skirt. There's not much I can do about her shirt except buy her a new one. Which of course I'll happily do.

January's smile is fond as she lets me take care of her, her hands finding my shoulders, my arms, my chest, as if she can never bear to let me go either.

I dip my head and kiss her again, because I can't resist that smile of hers. Can't resist any of her.

"There's something I should tell you about the meeting

tomorrow," I murmur into her throat. Lord, but her skin is soft.

"Mmm?" Pleasure is blurring her voice.

"Fuchs eats lunch every day at Roasted. Right when we'll be there."

She shoves herself upward and blinks down at me. "Oh. Oh, oh, oh."

"That's right."

"You'd better tell me your plan. All of it." Her next words are the sweetest I've ever heard. "We're in this together, after all."

CHAPTER 31

January

I'm exhausted, but there's enough caffeine and adrenaline running through me to have me vibrating in my chair at Roasted.

We're at ten minutes until Jack from Pixio is supposed to arrive, and I can't stop picking at my setup. There's our deconstructed phone, some slides for a short presentation on my laptop, and of course, Ultra running in the background, ready to impress.

I wriggle the connecting wire from the phone to the laptop. It doesn't seem that secure. Maybe I should—

Mark lays a hand over mine, his fingers brushing the tennis bracelet he gave me. He put that back on and the earrings last night, having carried them in his pocket all the way from Napa. "Stop. You'll undo all Doc's work."

That's exactly the thing to make me stop. Everyone worked so unbelievably hard last night, after everything I'd done...

I swallow and blink. My emotions are so on edge I'm bleeding just from breathing.

"And don't think about whatever you're thinking about." Mark hands me a handkerchief. "No tears. You're here because you're the smartest person working in encryption, Ultra is a game changer, and your team is amazing. And loves you."

I dab at my eyes. He's right—I can't let Jack see me like this, and I definitely can't let Fuchs. He's still not here yet, but Mark assured me he'll be arriving at twelve thirty on the dot.

So I've got to impress Jack and confront Fuchs. In fact, impressing Jack depends on confronting Fuchs.

"Are you sure you don't want to lead this?" I ask. This is Mark's specialty, not mine.

"Nope. You've got this. I'm only here as moral support."

He's the handsomest moral support I've ever seen. There's no sign of our sleepless night on his face. He's as confident, as languidly assured, as ever. I want to bottle his attitude and spray it on my wrists for courage.

He brings my hand to his lips. "I want to know what you're thinking about."

"Later." My cheeks are heating, half from embarrassment and half from desire. Probably the whole of the Silicon Valley elite is watching us, and I want to hide and preen all at once.

"That's a promise."

And then I see Jack walking across the café toward us, and my thoughts scatter. If I passed him on the street, I might not recognize him—he's got a middle-management dad vibe going on that doesn't at all fit with his position as the CEO of one of the largest tech companies in the world. I mean, there are many, many countries with economies smaller than Pixio's.

"Mark." He greets Mark with a smile and a shake, as if they're old friends. His clasp of my hand is shorter, his smile fixed. "And this must be January."

I'm guessing he's seen our pictures in *TidBytes* and he knows all about our relationship. But he's not giving any of that away in his expression. There's a reason he rose to where he is.

"Yep. And you must be Jack." I move myself closer into "friendly acquaintance" territory, the better to steel my nerves for this meeting. Mark is on my side, and Mark is his equal. Which puts me higher than I would be by myself. "Mark tells me you're interested in encryption."

He shrugs with one eyebrow. "Yeah, of course. We make it a priority at Pixio to keep data secure."

"And privacy. That's another interest of yours."

His expression flickers. "Privacy and encryption go hand in hand."

"I completely agree." I let my smile go dazzling. "Could I see your phone?"

"What?"

I don't let my smile slip. "A little demonstration. I promise I won't hurt it." His reaction is exactly what I was hoping for. He's acting like I'm asking to see his underwear, and when I show him what Fuchs has done to his precious, private phone... I'll have won him over then.

And after that, I'll let Ultra wow him and seal the deal. There's only one piece missing...

"Arne!" Mark pops up out of his chair and waves someone over. I don't turn around since a cold sweat has bloomed on my skin.

Jack swivels around, frowning. I keep smiling like this is totally normal.

"Arne is interested in cryptology too," Mark says, loud enough for Fuchs to hear. And about half the café. "He'll love this."

I refuse to look to see if Fuchs is coming. Part of me wishes he isn't so I won't have to face him, but I know we need him here if we want to finish off his spyware once and for all. I can't just sell Ultra—I have to stop him too.

When the sensation of something cold and slimy runs across my neck, I know that Fuchs has come over.

"Mark." It's flat but not combative. "Jack. It's good to see you, but I have my lunch meeting."

"No, you'll want to see this," Mark says. He's enjoying needling Fuchs, his stance easy yet alert. "Have a seat."

"Yeah," Jack says. "Join us." He thinks this is a meeting of peers, that Fuchs will want to hear this and have something valuable to add.

I need to pretend that's all that's happening here too. At least for right now.

"So could I see your phone?" I ask Jack again. "Just a small demonstration."

He stares at me for one long heartbeat, then pulls his phone out of his pocket, using his thumbprint to open it. He hangs on to it for the briefest second when he passes it over to me.

Perfect. He's very attached to this phone.

I look through the apps on the home screen. Bingo. He's got the PopPix app. I turn the phone back off and pass it to him.

"That's it?"

"Told you it would be quick." I toss him a smile and call up my command window that's running the Corvus program. "Did you know there's spyware in the PopPix app?"

His jaw tightens. "No, I didn't."

He doesn't believe me. So I turn the laptop screen around. "That's your camera phone right there, taking those images."

Jack's eyes go wide as he leans into the screen. The ceiling of the café is there, exposed pipes and concrete in the industrial chic fashion.

"What...?" He looks to his phone, which is still in sleep mode. With his forefinger, he nudges it. The images on the screen spin too. "How the fuck did you hack into my phone?

Not only is it password protected, the data is encrypted too."

The *fuck* he lets slip reveals how rattled he really is.

"This isn't a hack," Mark explains, his voice low. "This is the spyware she's talking about. It's in every major social media app now, ready to turn on cameras and microphones and GPS whenever the creator tells it to. And it can break the encryption that Pixio phones are currently using."

Jack isn't looking at Arne, not that Fuchs is giving any guilt away in his expression. Which is fine since we're not ready to nail him. Yet.

"If the images coming off your phone were encrypted by Ultra though," I say, "it wouldn't matter that spyware was trying to grab them. The thief would never see anything but noise." I hit the track pad with a flourish, calling up my program. "That's where Ultra comes in. The most powerful encryption system in the world."

I hold up the deconstructed phone. "We can't use your phone for this part of the demonstration because it's not running Ultra. But this is."

Once more, I start pulling video from the phone while it stays quiet and dark. Jack watches with hooded eyes.

And then I call Ultra into action, telling it to scramble the video.

Suddenly the image coming from the phone goes to white noise.

I release a breath. I hadn't realized how worried I was it wouldn't work until it did. "The spyware can't break my encryption. And nothing can be decoded without the user's unique key."

I demonstrate that for him too, showing him that Ultra can decode what it's already encoded. "See? No information has been lost. Just protected."

A muscle in Fuchs's jaw is twitching, his nostrils flaring as he fights for breath. Otherwise, all of him could be carved from ice.

His reaction frightens me—and makes me triumphant. He wasn't expecting anyone to be on to his plan, much less to be able to block him. But I and my team have outflanked him. We have *him* on the run.

Even if he is able to ruin my company, I'll remember this moment fondly. We've accomplished this, if nothing else.

I look to Mark, who's as assured and cool as ever. As if he never for a moment doubted that Ultra would work. Never for a moment doubted me.

I take a breath and draw on Mark's strength from across the table. We're in this together, and we've got this.

Finally I let myself look at Jack. His is the only reaction that really counts here.

Jack leans back, his eyes narrow and his shoulders closed off. I can't tell if he's impressed by Ultra or still shocked by the spyware. He taps on the screen of his phone. "How did you know about this?"

So he's focused on the spyware. I will myself to not be disappointed, but there's still a pinch in my middle.

"We can't tell you," Mark says. "But trust us, it's there and it's waiting. And this won't be the last attempt at something like this."

"Which we're ready for at Ultra," I say. "We're developing a chip that can generate new encryption codes based on machine learning. Put the Ultra system in all your phones, and you'll always be one step ahead of any attempt at data theft."

"January was on this way before anyone else," Mark says. The warmth in his eyes burns my cheeks. "She's the only person I'd trust to encrypt my data. She's… amazing."

I'm fighting my expression with all my might, but the love, the joy, is still seeping through, pulling up my cheeks, lighting my eyes, curving my mouth. It's the worst possible way to look at Mark while in a meeting with a high-powered CEO, but I can't help it. I love him too much.

"Thank you," is all I manage to say.

One of Jack's eyebrows twitches, but he otherwise doesn't comment. He steeples his fingers. "This is impressive. Let's set up a time for you to meet with some of my engineers, go over what you're doing in more detail."

Mark flashes me a grin. That's pretty close to a yes.

"Great," I say. "Anytime."

Mark shakes his head. Too eager. But he's still smiling. But hey, I've possibly just sold Ultra to Pixio, and I've let Fuchs know he won't get away with it. Oh, and I love Mark with all my heart. I can be a little overeager.

"I'm curious about the spyware though," Jack says. "Every social media app? How is that possible?"

Mark turns to Arne, who hasn't moved a muscle. "Well, Arne? How did you get them all to agree to it?"

Fuchs still doesn't move, although Jack has flinched in shock.

"Wait, what? Arne, this is your spyware?"

Fuchs slowly, deliberately folds his hand on the table. "You know I can't answer that. All of Corvus's projects are very sensitive. Top secret even."

"So you did do it. You fucking asshole."

I gasp. The CEO of Pixio has just called the CEO of Corvus a *fucking asshole* in my hearing. It's like having the president call the chief justice of the Supreme Court an asshole right in front of you.

Mark steps in. "We knew you would have concerns about this," he says to Jack. "Which is why we brought Ultra to you first."

"Concerns? You're goddamn right."

Fuchs snorts, the first show of any real emotion from

him. "Don't be a child. You've put a device in everyone's hand that tracks and records their every move. Of course someone's going to use that data."

"To do what?" I demand.

"Stop crime. Terrorist attacks. Track criminal networks and break them." Fuchs is sneering at me. "Stop governments who'd do our citizens harm."

"At the expense of everyone in America's privacy?" I ask. "You don't need to track everyone to do that." I'd say something about how it's also probably illegal, but I'm not entirely sure it is, and I don't think Fuchs would care.

He doesn't answer me. Apparently I'm not worthy of a response.

"So you *are* tracking phones?" Mark asks.

Fuchs won't be drawn in though. "I never said that. I said that someone is going to use that data if it's there."

Meaning Fuchs will. He doesn't have any qualms at all.

"You know what Pixio's stance on privacy is," Jack says flatly. "What our stance has always been. This violates all that."

"You only make the hardware. What do you care what software is on it?"

"Because people trust us!"

"And the government trusts me to keep track of things," Fuchs says.

Things, not people. I imagine we're all pixels on a screen to Fuchs.

"I can't allow this." Jack is shaking his head.

"The government will though." Fuchs is certain of that.

We've come to a standoff. None of them will say anything publicly because they don't want the attention from the media or the government, but privately...

I think I might have started a war between Pixio and

Corvus, a private little war. With Mark and the Bastards as a guerrilla force.

Fuchs rises suddenly. "Good luck, Miss Harris."

I can tell he hasn't forgotten his promise to ruin my company. But with Pixio's backing, Ultra won't be vulnerable. And he knows that and it enrages him.

"I have to get to my meeting," he says as he walks away.

The temperature rises five degrees once he's gone. I can finally take a full breath.

Jack is looking at both of us skeptically. "You had all this planned, didn't you?"

Mark is unabashed. "It's my job to know people and how they'll react. I knew Fuchs would be here, and I knew how you'd react to our demo."

Jack shakes his head. "You've hooked up with quite the character," he tells me.

"He's not a character," I say, never looking away from Mark. "He's... he's just Mark. Always has been."

I can tell Mark hears everything I can't say in front of Jack, because his cheeks darken a tinge. Almost like a blush but more manly.

When Jack shakes my hand this time, it's longer, firmer. I've been accepted. "My assistant will contact you to set up a meeting with our engineers and me. I'm dying to get a good look at the inside of your encryption system."

Only when he's gone do I let out my squeal. "Oh my God, oh my God, oh my God."

Mark drapes an arm over my shoulder, pulling me as close as the silly chairs will allow. If only we were in a booth. "I knew you'd do amazing. You're magnificent."

"But with Fuchs here and showing them both the spyware and Ultra..." I gesture, trying to encompass what we've just done. "And you were amazing too. It could have gone wrong at so many points."

His lips brush my temple. I don't care if the entire café is staring now; I lean into him, drawing in his warmth, his confidence, his love. "But it didn't."

"He'll be at the meeting with the engineers. Jack himself," I explain. "Do CEOs do that?"

"Told you he was interested in encryption. And no, he doesn't. You're special." He rises, tugs at my hand. "Let's get out of here and celebrate."

"We should invite my team and all the Bastards. And Anjie. This is as much their victory as ours."

"First we celebrate alone." He puts his mouth to my ear. "They won't miss us for another few hours."

I race him to the car.

CHAPTER 32

January has some bubbles on the tip of her nose, and it's killing me.

I reach out of the water—we're in the hot tub in my bathroom, relaxing after our victory today—and wipe them off. She giggles, the sound bright with the champagne we've been drinking.

Cold champagne, hot suds, and the woman I love—I can't imagine needing anything else in my life.

Scratch that. What I need is this woman in my life forever.

I pull her closer, our legs tangling. But I need to see her eyes for this.

"What do you want to do with Ultra now?" I hold up a hand when she starts to answer. "What you *really* want to do, not what you think your investors want."

Her expression goes still. She's beautiful like this, deep in thought. Her hair is clinging to her neck and breasts, her skin is damp and glowing, and her eyes... I'm always struck by the blue of her eyes.

I'll have to find her some sapphires that exact color. It will take some time, but she'd love them.

"I want to keep Ultra as its own company," she says finally. "Not sell it to any one bigger but keep it for myself. I know it will be difficult, but that's what I want."

"Then that's what you'll have."

Fear flits through her eyes. "And Fuchs? He has promised to destroy me."

"I don't want you to ever worry about him again. You concentrate on Ultra, and we'll take care of him." I squeeze her hand, which is slippery with the rose-scented suds enveloping us. "You're not alone now. You'll never be alone again."

All of her relaxes, and my ego roars. *That's right, honey. Leave everything to me. I'm strong enough to handle it, to fight your battles for you.*

Her foot slips up my thigh. "And what do you want?" she asks. It's clear what she has in mind.

But even though my cock responds, that's not what I quite have in mind.

Here it is. I'd told her once in college, but those were superficial requests: a date, a movie. The faint start of a romance.

We've come so much further now. And I want so much more.

I lean forward and kiss her, keeping it shallow when she demands more. I've already given her three orgasms tonight, and as much as I love her greedy desire, I need to finish this.

"I want you," I say against her lips. "I want you for always. I want you to move in with me. I want you to marry me. I want you by my side, in my heart, every second of every day."

I'm greedy too. Her eyes widen, and the tips of her breasts brush my chest as she pulls in a hard breath.

"Oh, Mark." Never has my name sounded sweeter on her lips. "I want you too. Exactly like that."

"Good. Because I'm going to take you. You're mine now."

Her smile is both knowing and accepting. Well, I always warned her I was a greedy bastard. But now I'm her bastard, completely and totally.

Which means I'll have to get Anjie on a moving company ASAP. All of January's things need to be in my house by the end of tomorrow. And then she never needs to leave again.

I spin her around and pull her back against my chest, ready to move on to the orgasm portion of this. I nip at the place where her neck meets her shoulder.

"First you're going to take tomorrow off," I say.

"What?" Indignation has to fight past the pleasure in her voice to get out. "I can't, not with—"

I bite a little harder this time. "You can. Just one day, the two of us going wherever we want. We'll wake up tomorrow and just go."

Her head falls back as she surrenders. "Where will we go?"

"Anywhere the car can take us. Or anywhere the jet can take us."

"You have a private jet." It's not a question.

"What kind of master of the universe would I be without a jet?"

"Hmm. Well, I don't care what kind you are, as long as you're mine."

"Done," I promise, sealing the best deal I've ever made.

CHAPTER 33

January

Six months later

There are no flourishes for encryption programs. The excitement is reserved for smartwatches and earbuds and laptops thinner than a credit card. Encryption is not what the masses want.

But I know it's what they need, so when at their annual product rollout, the CEO of Pixio announces an exciting development in encryption, provided by Ultra Systems, that will be available on every Pixio phone, I shout in the office we share. Mark splits his time between Ultra and the Bastards now, more often than not doing his deals from the desk right next to mine. He wasn't kidding about wanting to be with me every second of every day.

Mark looks over at me from his workstation, a huge smile on his face. "Are we celebrating tonight?"

As if our life together doesn't feel like one big celebration every day. Mark does more than pamper me—he cherishes me. All that stuff that a girl could get used to? I'm still not used to it, but I am enjoying it.

"We sure are," I say.

"Good, because I just got some other good news." He leans back in his chair. "Corvus has just quietly announced they're shuttering their Spiderweb project."

"What?" I drop my tools and rush over to him. Sure enough, there's the press release. They don't say anything about Spiderweb being the official name of their spyware division or that they've already tried to put it on a bunch of phones, but I can read between the lines.

Fuchs is still around, still a threat, although he hasn't done anything since our meeting with Jack, and Grace's immigration status is still up in the air, but we're winning. Slowly, but it's happening.

Outside my office, I hear my team whooping. I stick my head out. "Doc, open that champagne in the fridge."

Several hours later, when we've got all the celebrating out of our system and I've sent my team home, Mark and I return to my office.

Sitting on my workbench is the machine we've been working on for weeks together, waiting for us to finish it.

"Do you want to do this tonight?" Mark asks.

"Yeah. It feels… right."

So I connect one last wire, then step back. Here comes the big moment. I'm almost more frightened than when I presented Ultra to Pixio, even though the stakes are so much lower.

But are they? The machine sitting in front of me has a lot of symbolic importance to me and Mark. If it doesn't work, if we haven't assembled it properly, does that mean we're doomed?

No, of course not. We love each other too much for that to be true. But I'm still anxious about this.

"Do you want to do one last check?" he asks me, sounding as nervous as I feel.

Yes. I'm not ready for this.

But I was. "No, let's hit it."

I look at the message we've prepared and take a deep breath.

I press one of the keys. An *H*. There's some clicks and whirrs and then a key slams down, pressing an *A* into the paper. I hit another key, this time an *E*. More clicks and whirrs as the circuits flash and the tumblers turn. This time the *Y* key slams down, putting a *Y* right next to the previous *A*.

When we're done, our original message is just gibberish. Completely incomprehensible.

I smile so wide when I see it my mouth hurts.

"That's amazing," Mark says over my shoulder.

"Let's see if we can decode it."

I carefully set the tumblers to decode the message. Letter by letter, I type it back into the machine.

Hey, does this thing even work? is printed out when I'm finished. Exactly what I'd originally typed in. I pull the sheet out and start to laugh.

Mark hands me another sheet, gibberish on that one too. "Let's try this one." He's way too serious.

Suddenly my heart starts to race. But I set the tumblers and begin to type. With every letter that's added, my heart picks up speed until it's echoing in my ears.

January Harris, I love you with all my heart. Will you marry me?

I'd known this would be coming at some point—Mark hasn't exactly been shy about his intentions—but when he pulls a ring out of his pocket, rose gold with a diamond large enough to announce itself but not shout about it, I'm shaking.

This is all so real, his love for me, my love for him, that

236

I'm overwhelmed by it. It's too much emotion for one person to feel.

Thank God I've got Mark to feel it with me then.

"Of course," I say, my voice shaking as hard as I am. "Of course I will. I love you and—"

He's kissing me then, hard and demanding, and I know he's as moved as I am. Somehow he manages to slip the ring on my left hand.

I don't bother to look since I already know the ring is perfect. I keep kissing this perfect man of mine instead.

ABOUT THE AUTHOR

Raleigh fell in love with billionaire romance as a teenager thanks to Harlequin Presents. She fell in love with San Francisco in her twenties thanks to how charming the city was. And she fell for a coding genius thanks to how charming *he* was.

Naturally, she had to put all of the things she loved into her romances.

You can find her online at www.raleighdavis.com.